BETWEEN
WAR AND PEACE

PAT PATTEN

BETWEEN WAR AND PEACE

Copyright © 2025 by Pat Patten

Published by Patten Publications

This is a work of historical fiction. While inspired by actual events and real people, certain names, characters, places, and incidents are either the product of the author's imagination or used fictitiously for narrative purposes.

For media and publishing inquiries:
Patten Publications
P.O. Box 50541
Jacksonville Beach, Florida 32240

Cover and book design by Pat Patten

FIRST EDITION

Printed in the United States of America
ISBN: 979-8-9989937-0-1 (trade paperback)
ISBN: 979-8-9989937-1-8 (epub)

CONTENTS

DEDICATED TO

Jesus Christ and His Blessed Mother Mary

In gratitude for the mercy that sustained me,
the courage that carried me,
and the grace that made this work possible.

History remembers ordinary people
who do extraordinary things.

PAT PATTEN

CHAPTER 1

Crack the Whip

APRIL 23, 1782

It was a damp April evening in Middleborough, Massachusetts. Four young men huddled around a battered table in Sproat's Tavern, whispering about scandal. They hadn't lived long enough to know the true cost of shame.

"Three days ago, my grandmother saw a woman—dressed like a man—trying to join the army," said Harley Weems, teetering on the back legs of his ladder-back chair.

"Who?" asked Edward Harris.

"Deborah Sampson," Harley said. "She signed Israel Wood's enlistment book under the name Timothy Thayer. My grandmother saw the whole thing. Said the way she held the pen gave her away. Sampson's got a crooked finger from an old break and writes at a strange angle."

"What happened after that?" asked Brian Gill.

1

"Wood gave her half the bounty up front. But when it came time to muster, Timothy Thayer never showed. Grandma told Wood she was sure it was Sampson in disguise."

"That's fraud," Joe Smith muttered. "She could be thrown in jail."

"She denied everything," Harley said. "Told it straight to Wood's face. Even stood her ground in front of Pastor Allen and half the town council. No proof—just an old woman's word against hers."

"So, what happens now?" asked Brian.

"They want to punish her either way. She's got to return the bounty and stand before the Baptist congregation to confess. Pastor Allen says she's banned from the church unless she repents. The council's even talking jail if she refuses."

"Serves her right," Joe sneered. "A woman dressing like a man—that's a crime and a sin."

"It's unnatural," Brian added. "She needs to remember that God made women to serve men, not imitate them."

Upstairs, the treadle of a loom stilled.

Deborah Sampson sat rigid on her stool. Voices had crept up through a crack in the floorboards. She tried to keep weaving, but her hands refused to move. Shame had already taken hold—hot, sharp, and rising—like a fire she couldn't smother.

It was true. She had enlisted. And she'd seen Harley's grandmother, sitting in a corner of the pub carding wool, watching as she signed the articles of agreement.

The next day, when it came time to muster with the troops, she'd hidden in the woods until the muster was finished. A search party had come looking for her at Captain Benjamin Leonard's house, where she was staying at the time. Israel Wood, Harley's grandmother, and half the town council came to accuse her of the crimes of dressing as a man and trying to join the army. She'd denied it all. They had no proof. They'd never get it. She'd vanish before she'd bow to their demands.

Below, Edward Harris said, "That's odd behavior, even for a plain woman like her."

"She's no chance of finding a husband," Harley added. "Especially if she's pretending to be a soldier!"

"You arrogant pigs," Deborah muttered. "Not every woman's chasing a husband."

Another round of laughter erupted below.

"That's it," she snapped. "Guilty or not, I've had enough of them mocking me."

She stood, the stool screeching across the floor. Her fingers curled around the coiled whip at her side, braided leather, her own work, a symbol more than a weapon.

She descended the stairs, each step striking the boards like a hammer. The room hushed. Heads turned.

Then—crack.

The whip split the air like musket fire. The four young men froze; faces drained of color.

Deborah stood tall and unflinching, her blue eyes blazing.

"I'll thank you," she said, "to stop spreading lies about me."

3

Silence.

"Not every woman hunts for a husband. I live by my rules, not yours. I thank God He made me plain—beauty fades, but strength endures. I'd sooner walk alone than be with a man who sees himself as my master."

Gasps rippled through the room. No one laughed.

"One day," she said, her voice rising, "women will walk this earth as free as any man—free to think, to choose, to act. And none of you—not your councils, nor your laws—will stand in our way."

She coiled the whip, turned, and left. The door slammed behind her. Silence clung to the tavern like smoke.

At a corner table, four members of the town council sat nearby. Amos Prout spoke up. "Did you see that? Looked like she meant to flog them."

"She'd have managed it," Pastor Allen said. "She's taller than any of them and twice as strong."

"A woman like that needs a husband to bring her to heel," Prout said. "Remind her who's master."

Allen's eyes lit up. "Ephesians 5:22 says, Wives, submit yourselves unto your own husbands, as unto the Lord."

"She's guilty," Prout continued. "Dressed as a man and tried to enlist. Tonight's little outburst may have given us what we need to finally put her in her place—and force a confession."

"What do you have in mind?" Allen asked.

Prout grinned. "We'll find her a husband and draw up a marriage contract she can't refuse to sign."

4

"And who would marry her?" Allen asked.

"I know just the man," Prout said. "William Bennett. He's a neighbor of Reverend Thomas. Deborah worked for them ten years—Bennett saw plenty of her. And he's been hunting for a wife for quite some time now."

"I should think it would take quite a bit of convincing to get him to agree to marry her," said Allen.

Prout smiled. "With the right incentives, I think he can be persuaded to propose to Miss Sampson."

"What makes you think she'll accept his proposal?" Allen asked.

Prout leaned in, "She marries him or rots in jail."

Allen grinned. "What an excellent plan!"

"I'll speak to William tomorrow," Prout said, grinning.

And the trap was set.

CHAPTER 2

The Proposal

S pring had crept into Middleborough with a whisper of blooming lilacs and warm breezes stirring the tall grass. But that gentle peace shattered the moment Deborah walked through the front door of her lodgings, one week after the scene she had made at Sproat's Tavern.

The house was owned by Captain Leonard, a militia officer, and his wife Hannah.

Holding out a letter clutched in her brown hand, Jennie, Hannah's maid, was waiting.

"Miss Hannah said to give this to you the minute you came in."

Deborah cringed. She could see immediately it was from her mother, Deborah Bradford Sampson, who lived in Plympton, Massachusetts, eight miles away, where young Deborah was born.

"Well, that didn't take long," Deborah said to Jennie. "I'm pretty sure my mother is writing to chastise me for the cross words I had with Harley and his mates."

She opened the seal on the envelope and began to read.

"No! No! No! She can't do this to me."

"What's it say?" Jennie asked.

Deborah's face flushed with fury. "It seems my mother has been paid a dowry of twenty pounds by William Bennett to marry me."

Jennie's eyes widened. "Ain't you happy to be gitten' a husband?"

Deborah let out a bitter laugh. "No!"

Jennie flinched. "But a husband will take care of you for the rest of your life."

"I can take care of myself."

She scanned the rest of the letter. "Mother says Mr. Bennett will come to collect me on May 1st. That's tomorrow!"

Just then, Hannah Leonard came into the room. "I understand congratulations are in order."

"You read my letter?" Deborah asked.

"I mistook it for one from my sister, a harmless mistake. Surely you're pleased?"

"I am not going to marry Mr. Bennett. I've known him for years. He's a drunken, lazy, worthless pig of a man."

Hannah's expression soured. "Nevertheless, your mother has signed a legal contract binding you to Mr. Bennett."

"My mother does not own me and she has no say in my life anymore. I'm twenty-two years old, of legal age, and she can no longer sell me to anyone, as she has done repeatedly since I was five-years old. I can now make my own decisions about my life, and marrying Mr. Bennett is not one of them."

"It sounds to me that you have no choice, Deborah. You're obligated to marry him."

"I most certainly will not. I'm a masterless woman with my own income. For that contract to be valid, I would also have to sign it and agree to the terms, which I will never do!"

Jennie spoke up. "What you gonna' do when he comes tomorrow?"

"I'll tell him I'm not for sale, his contract is worthless, and to bugger off!"

She stormed off to her room and slammed the door. Sitting on her bed, Deborah wondered, *Who's behind this? It can't be mother; she doesn't even know Mr. Bennett.*

That night, after settling Hannah for bed, Jennie knocked softly on Deborah's door.

"Miss Deborah, you still awake?"

"Yes. Come in Jennie."

"What you goin' to do 'bout Mr. Bennett?"

Deborah shook her head. "I'm not sure. Don't you worry about me. I'll be fine."

"Okay. I'll pray for you all the same."

"Thank you, Jennie. Your prayers are much needed and greatly appreciated."

The next afternoon, just as the town clock struck four, a sharp knock rattled the front door. Jennie answered it and stepped back, startled.

A man stood swaying on the threshold, as round as he was tall, with a patchy beard. His suit, once the pride of another decade, hung limp and threadbare, reeking of stale ale and unwashed flesh. He tipped a grimy hat, though it nearly fell from his hand.

"Hello, sir," Jennie said.

"Afternoon. I'm here for Miss Deborah Sampson," he slurred.

"Sorry, sir. She's not here. May I ask who's calling?"

"William Bennett. I believe she's expecting me."

William had spent the better part of the day at Sproat's Tavern, trying to fortify his nerves with cider. The town council had convinced him that he was doing God's work, and theirs, by marrying Deborah. They'd even paid half the dowry, and had one of their own, a lawyer, draft the marriage contract.

Hannah Leonard appeared at the door, pushing Jennie aside. She put her fan to her face to cover her expression of shock at seeing Mr. Bennett. *Oh well, this is the best Deborah will ever get*, she thought to herself.

Hannah wasn't about to let this smelly little man into her house and sit on her damask covered sofa.

"I expect she'll be home in time for supper at five o'clock. Perhaps you'd like to come back then."

William nodded gratefully and tottered off to refill his courage.

Five o'clock chimed. Deborah came through the door for dinner. She was relieved to see there was no horse or buggy tied up outside the house.

Jennie met her at the door. "Mr. Bennett was here looking for you. Miss Hannah told him to come back at five, as you were expected for dinner."

As if summoned by fate, the door boomed with a loud knock. Wanting to get this over as quickly as possible, Deborah opened the door.

"Mr. Bennett," she said coolly.

"Good afternoon Miss Sampson. I've come with…"

"I know why you've come and I am afraid I must disappoint you. My mother had no right or claim to sell me in marriage to you. I am not for sale to you or any other man. Do I make myself clear?"

He waved a parchment in her face. "I have a legal contract that says otherwise. You will marry me tomorrow and there is nothing you can do about it."

"Is that so? Hmm, may I see the contract in question?"

She snatched it, scanning its contents. The town council had ordered her arrest if she refused to sign the contract. The incident at Sproat's had been twisted to label her a public menace.

The last paragraph was to do with her mother and the dowry she was to receive. Her mother's signature was clearly legible.

"The choice is clear; you either marry me or go to jail for an undetermined period. A jail is no place for a woman. You'd be much better off with me."

"Is that so? What makes you say that?"

He grinned. "I am a man of some means. I have a decent house, a cow, several chickens, and a horse."

"Why do you want to marry me Mr. Bennett? This clearly was not your idea."

"That is true. However, the town council convinced me that you'd make a good wife and that you currently support yourself. I would not object to you continuing to earn money."

"Money which I would then be legally required to turn over to you."

"Of course. As your husband, your money would become mine. Besides, what use would you have of it as I would be providing for all your needs."

Inside, Deborah was seething with rage but restrained herself from pummeling the little man and throwing him out the door. That would surely bring the sheriff round to take her to jail for assault.

"I don't see where I'm supposed to sign. Is my signature not relative to this contract?"

"No. It is not. Your mother is still your legal guardian, as you're unmarried. According to this contract, you belong to me, and the dowry has already been paid to your mother."

"Twenty pounds is quite a generous sum of money. I'm a bit surprised you had that kind of money on hand."

"Well, the town council paid half."

"How very generous of them."

"They were quite adamant that it would be best for you, me, and the community if you had a husband, basically someone to keep you in-line, so to speak."

"And that would be you," she laughed.

"That's right. If you do as you're told, you can sleep in the house. Otherwise, you'll be sleeping in the barn till you come to your senses and learn to obey me."

"What about children?"

"Of course, that's the most natural thing for you to do."

"How many children?"

"Four sons would be satisfactory."

She tilted her head. "And if the Almighty sends only daughters??"

Bennett gave a short, dismissive snort. "Surely, a big strong woman such as yourself would be inclined to have sons. Although one or two daughters, along with at least two sons, would be acceptable."

"I must admit, I have always dreamed of having a husband and children, but never once did I imagine my husband would be chosen for me by the town council."

"They're wise men," Bennett replied with smug assurance. "You'd do well to honor their judgment. I'll be an excellent father."

"What a promising future you paint for me. Let me see if I have this right. As long as I'm a good girl and do exactly as you say, I'll be allowed to cook, clean, take care of you, your house, and your animals, earn my own money, which I don't get to keep but must give to you, and bear you four children, preferably sons. And I do it all so that you and the town council can sleep at night safe in the knowledge that I won't cause any further trouble. Have I missed anything here?"

"No. You have summed up your duties quite accurately. If you do as you're told, you will have a very satisfying life."

"But I already have a satisfying life."

"In time, you'll come to realize that you're much better off with me."

Deborah needed time to think. She knew that if she flatly refused him he'd bring the town council and the sheriff back to force her to marry him or take her to jail.

"This is all a bit overwhelming. I'm in need of a rest to take it all in."

"I understand. I shall be back at 10:00 a.m. to collect you. Pastor Allen will be at the church ready to marry us."

"I have such a lot to do between now and then. Could we make it in the afternoon at 2:00pm?"

"Well, I will have to confirm that Pastor Allen's schedule will not conflict with a change in the time for our wedding."

"I'm confident that his schedule will be open at that time."

"Alright then. I'll be back for you tomorrow promptly at 2pm. Be ready. I don't like to be kept waiting."

"Of course, I understand. Goodbye, Mr. Bennett."

"Until tomorrow, Miss Sampson." His words slurred slightly as he braced himself against the doorframe, the sour scent of ale hanging in the air. He tipped his hat in a clumsy gesture before lurching down the steps.

The latch clicked as the door closed behind him. Deborah pressed her palm flat against the wood, fighting the overwhelming urge to scream and smash the nearest chair to splinters. Instead, she forced her fingers to unclench, eased the door shut without a slam, and fled down the narrow hall. By the time she reached her room, she was trembling, the fury inside her pressing for release like steam against a sealed kettle.

Hannah and Jennie followed.

"How very exciting. We're here to help you get ready," Hannah said.

Deborah clenched her fists to tamp down the rage she was feeling inside.

"It's all so much to take in. I need to take a bath. Jennie will you help me get the hot water ready?"

"Yes, I'll get it boiling now." Jennie scurried out of the room, leaving Deborah alone with Hannah.

"Now Deborah, I know he's not much to look at. He smells of stale ale and his clothes need washing, but at least he has a house that will one day be yours. A man like that surely won't live to old age. Besides, you can clean him up, help him with his diet and who knows, you might even get to like him."

Deborah took a moment to remind herself that she and Hannah had become friends while living together these last few months. She turned away, clenched her teeth, held her breath and fought with all her might to speak in a civil tone to Hannah.

"I would be grateful if you and Jennie would leave me alone tonight. Please do not disturb me in the morning, as I shall be staying up late tonight packing my things and praying to God to give me strength to face what lies ahead."

"I understand completely," said Hannah.

Jennie returned. "Tub's ready, Miss Deborah."

Deborah nodded. "Thank you, Jennie. Now if you'll both excuse me, I must get ready."

"Since you probably haven't eaten all day, I'll leave some food out for you in the kitchen," said Hannah.

"That's very kind of you. I'll eat later."

Deborah stepped into the steaming bath and let the heat swallow her whole. Water closed over her head like a veil, muffling the world. She held her breath beneath the surface, not just to calm her nerves, but as if by staying submerged, she might delay the inevitable. She will not be here at 2:00 p.m. tomorrow. Of that, she was certain.

Afterward, wrapped in a threadbare robe and cocooned in the warmth of her bed, the tension in her limbs finally began to unravel. Exhaustion had crept in like a thief, and soon she was asleep.

That's when the nightmare came.

It seized her in the dark like a vice. Her breath quickened, her body stiffened, and then the scream tore from her throat before she even knew it had escaped. Her bedroom door flew open with a bang.

"Miss Deborah!" Jennie rushed to her side. She grabbed Deborah by the shoulders and gave her a firm shake. "Wake up! You're havin' a bad dream."

Deborah lurched upright, drenched in sweat.

It took her a moment to realize where she was. "Thank you for waking me, Jennie. I'm all right now."

"You were shoutin' like the devil himself had hold of you," Jennie said, brushing the hair back from Deborah's damp forehead. "Sounded like you were fightin' for your life."

"It was a terrible dream, indeed. I'm so sorry I woke you. What time is it?"

"Just after ten."

"Would you make me a cup of coffee? I think it might help."

"Course I will." Jennie gave her a soft pat on the shoulder and went to the kitchen.

Deborah pulled the blanket tighter around her shoulders and stared into the shadows.

This was the second time she'd had that dream, the exact same one, down to the last chilling detail. Once might be nothing, but twice? An omen, she thought grimly. But of what?

There was only one person she trusted to answer that question, Mr. Graham, the old schoolmaster. Like the Joseph of Scripture, Mr. Graham had a unique way of seeing things others did not. If anyone could make sense of her dream, it was him. She would seek him out tonight, before she left town.

When Jennie returned with the coffee, Deborah thanked her with a faint smile. Taking the warm cup into her hands, she drank in silence, the steam rising to meet her face as the hush of the house deepened. Jennie retired to bed, her footsteps creaking on the floorboards and vanishing into stillness.

But this time, Deborah did not sleep.

She waited, watchful, listening. Only when she was certain the house was silent did she move. Easing off the bed, she dropped to her knees and pulled a parcel from beneath the bed.

The bundle was wrapped in a faded linen cloth and tied with twine. Inside lay a complete set of men's clothing, each piece handmade with patient precision over the last year. She had woven every thread herself, working by moonlight and firelight, one secret stitch at a time.

There was a long white cotton shirt, soft but strong, and a pair of plain brown breeches. A pair of hand-knitted stockings were rolled up beside a thick wool coat, that had been dyed deep brown with walnut hulls. The hat, her pride and joy, was shaped from a scrap of tanned deerskin bought off a trapper, molded to fit her head and lined with wool.

This was the same outfit she had worn when she tried to enlist as Timothy Thayer and proved it was a convincing disguise.

She stripped off her nightdress and underthings. Then came the linen bandages, thin, tight strips she had woven to bind her chest. Her breasts were small, but small wasn't flat. And flat could mean the difference between safety and discovery.

The bindings were scratchy, but she didn't mind the discomfort. Each tug to tighten them was a declaration of freedom.

The shirt slipped over her head, falling loose across her shoulders. Breeches followed, snug and plain. Then the stockings, the waistcoat, then the overcoat, and finally, the shoes. They were a scuffed pair of men's leather shoes she had salvaged from a rubbish tip behind Sproat's Tavern. She had restored them using beeswax and polish until they shone like new.

Pulling the pins from her hair, her thick, straight, blond hair tumbled free. With practiced fingers, she combed through it, then tied her hair back with a narrow strip of black cotton. Later on, she'd cut it shorter when she was farther away from Middleborough, where no one would recognize her.

Crossing to the small mirror that hung beside her door, Deborah paused. A young man, lean and sharp-eyed, with a quiet confidence looked back at her. No chains, no vows. From now on, only freedom.

"Goodbye, Deborah Sampson," she whispered. "Hello, Robert Shurtlieff. But everyone calls me Bob."

She winked. "It's a pleasure to make your acquaintance, Bob."

Deborah had thought long and hard about the name. It needed to be common enough not to raise suspicion, and in Plymouth County alone, there were plenty of Shurtlieff's, some with an 'e,' some without. She chose to include it.

Levi and Mary Shurtliff lived just down the road from Reverend Thomas in Middleborough, and Deborah got to know them well. She had spent ten years, from the age of eight to eighteen, as the Reverend's indentured servant and helped raise all six of the Thomas boys.

The Shurtliff's had always been kind to her, smiling and nodding whenever she passed them on her way to the Third Baptist Church. They had joined just a month before she had. There was even a real Robert Shurtlieff in Carver, but Deborah had never met him. Should anyone ever question her origins, she could describe the town in detail, name streets and families, down to the way the sun struck the steeple in the morning. It would be enough.

Grabbing her satchel, she went into the kitchen, careful not to wake Jennie, who slept in a small room behind the pantry. Hannah had left out bread, cheese, and a small pouch of dried apples. Deborah packed the food quickly, tied the satchel shut, and slipped out the door just as the town clock struck midnight.

The night air was brisk against her cheeks, clean and full of promise. Above her, the stars stretched wide and endless. She tucked her hair beneath her cap, buttoned her coat tight, and caught a glimpse of herself in the darkened windowpane. This was it. There would be no turning back. From this moment onward, she would walk the world as Bob Shurtlieff.

As she walked away, she began to pray aloud, her lips barely moving.

"Guide me through the darkness ahead, Lord. You placed this fire in me to start a new kind of life. Give me the courage and determination to see it through. Let those who seek to bind me one day understand that I'm not a woman meant for chains but am here to serve a greater purpose and to do it with dignity and strength."

Deborah took one final look at the house, then turned down the lane toward the edge of town. Before she vanished into the night, there was one last stop she needed to make. She had to find out what the dream meant and what it might be warning her against. Only Mr. Graham would be able to tell her its meaning.

CHAPTER 3

The Dream

MAY 2, 1782 – 12:30 A.M.

Buried deep inside the ancient chestnut forest stood a dilapidated cottage on the outskirts of Middleborough. This was the first time Deborah, now Bob Shurtlieff, had ever traveled alone so far from home or stayed out so late. The thrill of it was dampened by a rising sense of dread. The dense blackness around him felt like drowning in a sea of tar, the trees pressing close, sealing off the moonlight. He walked along the ancient Indian trail, said to be prowled by highwaymen, murderers, and sometimes, runaway slaves heading for Canada.

The cottage belonged to the Grahams, once a beloved family in Middleborough. All three Graham boys had perished fighting under George Washington during the long War of Independence. Jacob Graham, though a year older than Deborah, had been a childhood friend.

23

The Grahams had immigrated from Cornwall, England twenty years earlier. William Graham, the patriarch, was a quiet man with a dangerous gift. A simple touch of a person or a personal belonging would open a vision of their future. He hid this ability well, though such secrets have a way of seeping through cracks.

When William held his firstborn, David, and later, Michael, he saw visions of their deaths in battle. Terrified, he uprooted his family and sailed to America in hopes of altering fate. But fate has a long memory.

William worked hard to build a new life in Middleborough. He and his wife raised their sons to be strong, but when they were grown, nothing could stop the pull of war. Despite their parents' pleas, David and Michael enlisted in the Continental Army and died at Monmouth. Jacob, grief-stricken, enlisted next. He died from measles complicated by pneumonia at Yorktown on the very day of Cornwallis's surrender.

The news of Jacob's death shattered Mrs. Graham. She died three months later. William withdrew from the world entirely. He no longer attended church, not even for his wife's funeral.

Once respected, William became a ghost among the living. The once tidy cabin decayed into ruin. The garden wilted, overrun with weeds. No one visited anymore. Those who did came by night and left in the shadows.

Now, Bob stood trembling at the weather-beaten door. He raised a hand to knock, but before his knuckles touched wood, the door swung open.

"Who are you, boy?" William growled.

"My name is Bob Shurtlieff. I was a friend of Jacob's. I'm very sorry for your loss, Mr. Graham."

William grunted, eyeing the stranger. His once handsome face had been ravaged by grief and neglect. Tangled gray hair fell past his shoulders. His eyes were hollow, black pits of sorrow.

"I don't remember Jacob mentioning you. Where are you from?"

"Carver, sir. We met at the market."

"Hmph."

"May I come in?"

William hesitated, then stepped aside. "Alright, as you were Jacob's friend."

The cabin was frozen in time. Bundles of herbs and flowers still hung from the rafters. The air was heavy with the mingled scent of decay and lavender. A magnificent four-poster bed stood draped in dusty linens. A ratty blanket near the hearth now served as William's bed.

"Why are you here?" William asked.

"I've had a dream. Twice. It frightened me, and I hoped you might help me to understand it."

William sighed. "Most want their future told. Few seek the meaning of dreams."

"But I believe it's tied to my future. I need to know what it means."

"When was the first time you had it?"

"April 15, 1775. Four days before Lexington. And again tonight."

"You think it came back for a reason?"

"Yes. I'm about to begin a journey. I think the dream is trying to tell me something."

"I will tell you what I can. But know this, I won't soften the truth."

"That is all I ask."

William pointed to a chair beside an old oak table where a chessboard sat ready, frozen mid-game. Bob sat carefully.

"Now," William said. "Tell me your dream."

Bob took in a deep breath, and then, slowly and deliberately, exhaled.

"I am watching the sun set on the hillside that overlooks a pleasant and fertile meadow filled with all manner of flowers and grasses. Herds are grazing, farmers are tending their fields, and a gentle breeze is blowing, wafting ravishing odors in my direction. As I stand there, my thoughts are turned to sublime ideas of Creation and that Being who has caused it all to exist. "

"What you describe is very much like the countryside that surrounds this cabin, a beautiful scene indeed. How is that frightening?"

"A sudden change occurs which invokes astonishment and horror. An immense darkness fills the sky and then begins incessant lightning and tremendous peals of thunder. I am overwhelmed with the stench of sulfur, the smell of Hell. The field disappears below a convulsing sea with mountainous waves. Ships are at once dashing against rocks and one another or foundering amidst the surges. The farmers have all fled for their lives. Then a volcano appears rising out of the ocean shaking with the perpetual roar of thunder. A hideous serpent rolls itself from the ocean, approaching me with great speed. I flee to my home and looking back, see the streets through which I passed are drenched with blood. At length I found myself in my own apartment. The door of the apartment opens of itself, and the serpent is there in a larger and more frightful form."

"Can you describe what the serpent looked like?"

"He was of immense bigness, his mouth opened wide and with teeth of great length. His tongue appeared to have a sharp sting in the end. He advanced toward my bedside, his head raised as nearly as I conjectured about five or six feet, his eyes resembled balls of fire. I was frightened beyond description. I covered my head and tried to call for assistance but could make no noise.

At length I heard a voice saying, 'Arise, stand on your feet, gird yourself, and prepare to encounter your enemy.' I rose up, stood upon the bed; but before I had time to dress, the serpent approached and seemed to swallow me whole. I called upon God for assistance and at that instant I beheld at my feet a bludgeon which I readily took into my hands and immediately had a severe combat with the enemy. The serpent turns to leave but as he does so he is lashing at me with a tail that resembled that of a fish, more than that of a serpent. It was divided into several parts and on each branch were capital letters of yellow gilt, saying what is not clear. I pursue him and strike till at length I dislocated every one of his joints, which fell into pieces on the ground."

"It sounds as if you destroyed this monster."

"Oh no sir, that is not the end of it."

"Pray, tell me the rest."

"The monster then reunites from the fractured pieces at my feet into an ox. He came at me a second time, roaring and trying to gore me with his horns. Once again I beat him off with my bludgeon, so that he fell into pieces on the ground. I ran to gather the pieces but found them nothing but a jelly and I immediately awoke."

"A most horrifying dream, indeed and yet filled with good omens."

"What does it all mean?"

"The serpent that rises from the flames is an omen that you will face great trials ahead. The fact that you destroyed the snake and all its subsequent forms means you will be victorious over your enemies. It shows you have inside you the power to shape your own life and be the kind of person you want to be."

Bob stood, his face alight with determination.

"Thank you, sir, for relieving my anxiety. What you have said gives me great confidence in the decisions I have made in order that I may follow my destiny and join in our country's fight for freedom."

William frowned. "Freedom means different things to many people. It comes with too high a price that will leave us all in chains, wallowing in the blood and ashes of our slain soldiers."

"Well sir, as Mr. Thomas Paine says, 'The sun never shined on a cause of greater worth.' I believe in it with all my heart."

William opened the door motioning for Bob to leave. "Good luck boy."

Bob paused. "Please, let me offer you some food, in thanks."

William arched a brow. "What do you have?"

"I have some bread, cheese, and dried apples."

"I will accept whatever you deem worthy."

Bob was so grateful, he handed William the parcel of food.

"Please sir, take all of it. I am sure I can get more."

William's finger lightly brushed Bob's hand. He looked closely at Bob's face and smiled.

"On second thought, you keep your food. I have no need of it now."

Bob blushed and turned to leave.

"You have the propensity for many uncommon enterprises that you have long held in suspension. It is important to remember you are only a victim if you think you are. This journey will shape the person you are about to become."

"Thank you so much. You have given me great hope for a better future. Goodbye sir."

As Bob glanced back, he saw William's face exuding the gray pallor of a man about to die. Bob knew his secret was safe for now.

William turned back inside. He lay down on the hearth blanket. A soft light filled the cabin. He felt himself rise, floating above his wasted body. A voice spoke gently.

"William, come. It's time to go home."

He turned. Jesus stood beside him.

Without words, He took William's hand and led him into the Light. There stood his wife with his sons, young, whole, waiting.

"Welcome home," they said, voices united without speaking.

Together, the Graham family walked through the gates of Heaven.

William looked once more at the Lord. "Thank you for bringing me home."

Jesus smiled. "Your work is done. My Father is well pleased."

And then they became the Light, one with the Love that is all things.

CHAPTER 4

Call Of The Sea

MAY 2, 1782 – 8:00 A.M.

After leaving the Grahams, Bob began the long walk under cover of night, weaving his way through the dense forest from Middleborough to the harbor at Bedford Village, twenty miles distant. Though fear lurked at the edges of his mind, it was swallowed by the stronger pulse of anticipation. The quest for freedom surged in his blood.

Bedford Village shimmered in the rising sun; its harbor painted in hues of orange and gold. Bob stood on the ridge overlooking the town and felt, for the first time, that he was standing on the edge of something vast and wondrous.

He headed towards the harbor. Scanning the ships moored along the wharf, one in particular caught his eye, the Argosy, a three-masted whaler bristling with activity. Sailors swarmed her decks, coiling ropes and loading supplies with practiced rhythm. Something about the ship buzzed with purpose. He made his way aboard.

A gruff voice met him. "Hello, boy. Welcome aboard. I'm Captain Carson. Who might you be?"

"Bob Shurtlieff, sir."

"What brings you to my ship?"

"I'd like to hire on as a deckhand."

"I need a cabin boy."

Bob nodded quickly. "That'll suit me fine, sir."

"Think you've got the salt for it? Life at sea's no holiday."

Bob drew a steadying breath. "Yes, Captain. I'm ready."

Carson gave a sharp nod. "Mr. Beecham, sign this boy onto the list."

The first mate, a lean, gruff looking man, opened the ship's log. "Mark your name here, boy."

Bob wrote his name into the log with quiet resolve.

"Ah, he can write," said Beecham, with mild surprise. "You're part of the crew now."

"That'll be useful," Carson replied. "Now, Bob, your first duty is to run down to the last warehouse on the pier and tell Mr. Hughes we're waiting on our supplies."

"Aye, Captain."

Bob ran down the gangplank. The warehouse loomed ahead, where a burly man wrestled with heavy barrels.

"Good morning, sir. Are you Mr. Hughes?"

The man straightened and wiped his brow. "Yes, I'm Sam Hughes. And who might you be?"

32

"Bob Shurtlieff. Captain Carson, from the Argosy, sent me. Says he's waiting for you to bring his supplies."

"Nice to meet you Bob," said Sam. "Is this your first time at sea?"

"Yes, sir. Is it that obvious?"

"Your eagerness gave you away," said Hughes. "Did you sign the crew book?"

"Yes, I did. Is there a problem?"

Hughes glanced over his shoulder, then leaned in. "Aye, there is. You're bound to the Argosy now. Captain Carson's no man to work under. He beats his crew for the smallest infraction. Good lads have died under his command."

Bob paled. "What should I do?"

"Run. Fast and far. I'll delay delivery for an hour, but after that, they'll be after you."

"Thank you, sir." Bob didn't hesitate. He bolted, pounding up the road into the forest. Terror lit a fire in his blood. Each stride tore him farther from the life he had nearly fallen into.

For an hour he ran. Then, the pounding of hooves echoed through the forest. Beecham and his men were on horseback, crashing through the woods and closing in fast.

Bob grabbed a leafy branch and swept it across his trail, erasing his footprints. A hill loomed ahead. He veered toward it, bounding off the path with a final leap, landing in the deep brush.

He crouched, breath ragged, moving silently through the undergrowth.

"There he is!" a voice shouted.

For a fraction of a moment, Bob froze, then sprinted deeper into the woods.

"Run all you want, boy. There's no escape. You're coming back with us, one way or the other."

Bob kept moving. He didn't know it yet, but fate was already running to meet him.

CHAPTER 5

A Hole In Time

MAY 2, 1782 – 10:00 A.M.

B ob kept running in the direction of a cluster of giant chestnut trees that seemed to stand out ahead. Just then, he heard a voice saying, "Come this way. Now!" The bushes inside the cluster of trees moved aside and a small man appeared standing next to a hole in the ground.

"Quick, jump in here," whispered the little man.

Bob responded instinctively and dove into the hole. The little man quickly covered up the entrance to the underground cave with a log and branches.

"Where'd he go?" asked the rider nearest to where Bob was last seen. "One minute he was there and the next he just disappeared."

The men scoured the area and could find no trace of Bob's footprints.

"Looks like we've been chasing a ghost. We best get back to the ship," said one of Beecham's men.

The little man and Bob listened as Beecham and his men left.

"I can't thank you enough, sir. You just saved my life," said Bob.

"What's your name, boy?" asked the little man.

"Bob Shurtlieff," sir.

"Mine's Toby Granger. Pleased to make your acquaintance."

As Toby lit a torch, the walls came alive with the movement of the light. Drawings of strange animals of all shapes and kinds took Bob's breath away.

"What is this place?" asked Bob.

"I believe it was a sacred place to people who must have lived here long ago. Many of the animals in the paintings no longer exist," said Toby.

"Why do you suppose they did this?" asked Bob.

"Natives today often talk about honoring the animals they are about to hunt. I think the idea is that drawing them in such a realistic way, as if they were here, keeps their spirit alive. It's a way to thank them for their sacrifice. The spirits of the animals give up their lives so the spirits of the people who kill them can live," said Toby. "It's a kind of circle of life. One life ends, another begins."

"I've never thought about that before, that animals might have a spirit. The pastor of my congregation would never even consider such an idea," said Bob.

"What's the name of the church you belong to?" asked Toby.

"Third Baptist Church of Middleborough," said Bob. "But I'm not a member anymore."

"Sounds serious," said Toby.

"It's a story for another day. Tell me where does this cave lead to?"

"It follows the path of an underground river for about ten miles north. Runaway slaves sometimes use this cave to escape on their way to freedom in the north," said Toby.

"How would they ever find this place?" asked Bob.

"They sew maps on quilts to show the way. Some that make it to Canada, come back to try to get their relatives out. They give them landmarks to follow. The slaves that stay behind sew the maps and show them to anyone who wants to try to escape. Their masters never figure out how the slaves always find their way north. It's all right there embroidered on quilts," said Toby. If you see quilts hanging outside a window, they appear to be drying, but they're actually showing escaping slaves where to go.

"That's amazing. How is it you know so much about the slaves and their escape routes?" asked Bob.

"Slaves all have the same prayer, to be free. I admire the courage and determination of those that risk everything to breathe in the fresh air of freedom, which is something we take for granted," said Toby. "So, I do whatever I can to help the ones that cross my path."

"You're a good man, Toby. I'm blessed to have met you," said Bob. "Maybe one day I'll have a chance to help a slave get to freedom."

"The Bible says three things will last forever: faith, hope, and love, and the greatest of these is love. I believe we all have the same purpose in life, to show love to all God's creatures," said Toby.

"Amen to that," said Bob. "No man, woman or child deserves to be held in bondage."

Toby and Bob continued walking down into the deep cavern where the wall drawings got bigger and more detailed. It was as if they were walking in an ancient cathedral with high ceilings.

"This place is a sanctuary, a place where people had worshiped their God of the hunt thousands of years ago. These ancient images are echoes of the past. Look here. See how they appear to come alive when touched by the light flickering on the walls," said Toby.

Bob felt their presence. The bison, with his enormous head and humpback, snorting and stomping his feet, bellowing a warning to the intruders about what lies ahead. The antelope, with his front and rear legs outstretched, not touching the ground, running in the wind. Many of the animals Bob couldn't identify, as they no longer existed. However, they all appeared to be alive, on the move, heading towards a rendezvous with their own sacrificial death in order to maintain the circle of life.

Bob gasped as he took in the scene. "This cave is magical."

"That's what the Natives believed," replied Toby.

Bob nearly tripped as his foot hit something on the ground that made a clinking sound. As he brought the torch close to the ground, a pair of iron shackles glinted in the light, still attached to the hands of the poor soul who died on this spot beneath Bob's feet.

"Oh, my goodness. I'm so sorry," said Bob apologizing to the skeleton.

"Although his hands were still imprisoned in iron cuffs, at least he died a free man," said Toby.

Bob knelt down and began to pray as he removed the cuffs from the bones of the dead man, flinging them aside. "Thank you Lord Jesus for bringing this man freedom and peace. Now that he has fled the darkness, I pray that he is embraced in Your everlasting arms, in the dawn of a new life. May he abide with You in the presence of God the Father forever."

Bob stood slowly, something within him changed. The weight of the shackles was no longer iron, but purpose.

"That's a mighty fine prayer," said Toby. "He almost made it too. The exit out of this cave is just ahead and Freetown is less than a mile away. There's several people there that would have helped him on his way."

"At least he's no longer shackled to what must have been a miserable life," said Bob.

Before exiting the cave, Toby took both torches and plunged the tips of fire into the sand and stood them up again.

"What are you doing?" asked Bob.

Pulling open his backpack, Toby pulled out a leather pouch, "I'm putting more bear grease on the torches, getting them ready for the next travelers."

"Won't they be going in the wrong direction?" asked Bob.

"Not for those headed south to help more people escape," explained Toby. "It's a small gesture but it will help to light their way through the darkness."

Toby carefully pulled apart the vines to exit the cave and made sure the entrance was once again hidden.

"Where are you headed now?" asked Toby.

"Boston," replied Bob. "How far do you think it is from here?"

"About fifty miles," said Toby. "This cave is part of the trail the Indians used to travel between the north and the south. Runaway slaves call it the Freedom Trail. It goes north, in almost a straight line, and passes through Boston Common.

"I can't thank you enough for saving my life and showing me the way to go," said Bob.

"Boston is a big place. Do you know anyone there?" asked Toby.

"Not really. I'm hoping to join Washington's army," said Bob.

"In that case, you'd do well to make your way to the Green Dragon Tavern on Green Dragon Lane," said Toby. "It's near Boston Common. You'll find people there that can help you."

"What sort of people?" asked Bob.

"It's the headquarters for the Sons of Liberty, and where Sam Adams and John Hancock planned and launched the rebellion against the British Stamp Act in '65. You may have read about it, they called it the Boston Tea Party," said Toby.

"Is it true they all dressed as Indians and painted their faces red?" asked Bob.

Toby chuckled. "Yes they did and they launched the raid from the Green Dragon. After the raid was over, they all returned to the pub and had a rip-roaring party that lasted through the night."

"I read they dumped 46 tons of tea into the harbor that night," said Bob.

"That's true. The fish all left the area and didn't come back for several days," remarked Toby.

"Sam and John, along with Paul Revere, still meet at the Dragon. They're on the planning committee for the war," added Toby. "Be sure to tell them I am doing well and wish them all the best."

"I'll do that. Thank you again for everything, Toby. I best be going," said Bob.

"Good luck on your travels, boy," said Toby. "I hope you find the kind of life and adventure you're looking for."

Bob wiped away tears. He'd never met anyone like Toby Granger, a stranger who truly cared about his life and future.

CHAPTER 6

Narrow Escape

MAY 5, 1782

A cool breeze brushed Bob's face, tempering the blaze of the midday sun. Withered leaves crunched beneath his feet as he followed a well-worn trail through a stand of aspen trees. Their golden leaves shimmered like lace curtains fluttering in a sunlit window. The entire forest pulsed with life, each tree and creature a vital part of the whole, as though the woods themselves breathed in harmony.

As he walked, Bob drew in the majesty of the land. He imagined the trees whispering, "Safe journey," through the wind. The scent of wildflowers perfumed the air, calling bees to drink from their nectar. Bluebirds, red cardinals, black crows, and orange-breasted robins flitting from branch to branch, their cheerful chirping a chorus of gossip high above his head.

"Could there be any place more beautiful than this?" he wondered.

With his long stride, Bob could walk five miles in an hour. With the extended light of late spring, he estimated he might cover thirty miles before nightfall. By dusk, tired and ravenous, he spotted the distant twinkle of village lights. Hope stirred in his chest as he made his way toward them, praying he could find food and shelter for the night.

The village, he soon realized, was Sharon. He recognized it as the home of his mother's sister, Alice Bradford Waters, and her husband, Zebulon. Morse Tavern was the only place in town offering both sustenance and lodging. Though it was a risk, hunger and exhaustion outweighed caution. He would take the chance.

The pub was impossible to miss. Light blazed from its windows, and the air was thick with the sounds of fiddles, clapping, and drunken laughter. The two-story structure pulsed with life. Bob pulled his hat low, slipping through the door and heading straight for the bar.

"Evenin', stranger. What'll you have?" the tavern-keeper called over the din.

"A pint of cider, a hot plate, and a bed—if you've one free. In that order," Bob said.

"Aye, you'll have it." The man vanished toward the kitchen.

Bob slipped into a corner table where the shadows gathered, keeping both doors in sight. He drew his hat brim low, scanning the room with a cautious eye.

Soon the keeper returned with a tankard of cider, a bowl of stew, and a heel of bread.

"That'll serve," Bob said, setting to quickly as if the meal might vanish if he tarried.

When he finished eating, he climbed the stairs hoping to get some sleep. The room was large but crude, lit only by a single candle on the windowsill. Several men were already sprawled across the floor, sleeping on straw mattresses. The air was rank with the stench of vomit and urine. As Bob entered, he overheard two men in the corner engaged in an animated conversation.

"What brings you to Sharon?" one of the men asked.

"I'm looking for my future wife," the other replied. "She ran off after I proposed. Has kin around here, so I reckon she came this way."

"She pretty?"

"No. Pretty women are nothing but trouble. This one's tall, homely, long chin. Strong as an ox, and stubborn too. But I'll beat that out of her soon enough."

"And if she won't go with you?"

"I already paid her mother a fair price. She's got no choice. She'll be my wife whether she likes it or not."

The voice was arrogant—and familiar. A chill ran through Bob. It was William Bennett.

Bob gasped, stumbled back, and tripped over a man snoring by the door. He hit the floor, scrambled up, and bolted—half falling down the stairs, shoving through the crowd. He burst into the night air, his chest pounding.

"Why d'you suppose that feller left in such a hurry?" the second man muttered.

"That was her," Bennett growled. "Get her!"

Bob heard his voice cut through the din: "Deborah Sampson, you come back here!"

They lurched after him as fast as their drunken legs could manage.

"Did a tall, lanky fellow with fair hair just bolt through here?" Bennett barked at two men by the door.

"Aye," one said. "Ran like the devil was at his heels."

Bennett and his companion staggered out into the dark, shouting her name into the night. But Bob was already gone, swallowed by the woods.

He ran until the shouts faded, until only the sounds of the forest remained. A full moon cast a silver sheen on the trail, the North Star steady above. He followed it like a beacon of freedom.

Breathless, Bob finally slowed. Tears stung his eyes, but he didn't stop. "I'll never be a slave to any man," he whispered.

The forest screamed with life around him. Male cicadas shrieked their mating calls, scraping their tymbals into a deafening buzz. Vixens cried like haunted women, though they sought, not fled, their mates. Frogs yelped, bats clicked, and owls screeched in the darkness. The cacophony was wild, unrelenting.

But Bob kept going. No matter how tired he was, he could never sleep with such noise or fear breathing down his neck. So he moved forward, toward freedom, and whatever lay beyond the trees.

CHAPTER 7

Weight Of Shame

MAY 6, 1782 – 7:00 A.M.

B ob followed the Freedom Trail and arrived at the heart of Boston Common, just as the distant bell tower tolled seven. There, in the center, stood a great elm tree, ancient and alone, its branches outstretched, presiding over the land.

At its base, a woman sat on a worn bench. Her frame was frail, her once-elegant clothing now faded and threadbare. An open journal rested on her lap. Her skin, once smooth and dark as polished obsidian, had taken on a dusty pallor, but her soulful eyes glinted in the morning light.

"Good morning to you, sir," she said with a gentle smile.

Bob hesitated. Most of the Black men and women he had encountered rarely spoke first to whites.

"May I share your bench?" he asked.

She chuckled softly. "It is not my bench, sir. Anyone may sit here."

He settled beside her. "I keep a journal as well, though I confess I haven't had much time for writing lately."

"I find early mornings perfect for it. The quiet is good for thoughts. I write poetry, stories, whatever visits me."

"You're a poet?" Bob brightened. "That's a skill I've never managed. I'd be honored to read your work someday."

"It's possible you already have," she replied, closing her journal with care. "I am Phillis Wheatley Peters. I wrote a letter and a poem to General Washington once. It was published in the American Monthly Museum, back in '76."

Bob stared. "You're Phillis Wheatley?"

"I was. Now I am Mrs. Phillis Peters."

"I believe you're one of the greatest writers of our time," he said earnestly.

She smiled, though, with a touch of sorrow. "Thank you. Few in this country would agree."

"Oh, but one day they will. I'm certain of it. Forgive my manners, Bob Shurtlieff, ma'am. What an honor it is to meet you."

"The pleasure is mine, Mr. Shurtlieff."

"Are you writing a new poem?" he asked.

"Yes. I've only just begun. I call it Liberty and Peace. It's inspired by General Washington's victory at Yorktown."

"Would you share a little of it?"

She nodded and read aloud from her journal:

LO! Freedom comes. Th' prescient Muse foretold,
All Eyes th' accomplish'd Prophecy behold:
Her Port describ'd, She moves divinely fair,
Olive and Laurel bind her golden Hair.
She, the bright Progeny of Heaven, descends,
And every Grace her sovereign Step attends;
For now kind Heaven, indulgent to our Prayer,
In smiling Peace resolves the Din of War.

"That's beautiful," Bob said quietly. "Your ability to say so much using a few, but precisely chosen words, is what I greatly admire about your writing."

Phillis smiled. "That's very kind of you to say."

"Thank you so much for sharing your latest masterpiece with me. I look forward to reading the finished poem."

"It will be some time before it's published," she replied.

"I truly am one of your biggest fans." Excitedly, Bob opened his rucksack and pulled out his journal. "You see here, I clipped the letter and poem you wrote to George Washington from the paper. I always carry it with me. Your letter and poem were the inspiration for my own quest for freedom."

"Freedom from what?" asked Phillis. "You don't appear to be a slave, and by all appearances, are already a free man."

"My mother sold me at the age of five into servitude. I've had a variety of masters, all of whom have held me back, one way or another, preventing me from being able to choose my own path in life," explained Bob.

"You cannot possibly equate your indentured servitude with that of millions of my own African brothers and sisters held in slavery in the most appalling conditions. They will never have a chance to choose their path in life. What you said is an insult to us all." Phillis closed her journal and stood up in a huff to leave.

"Please, forgive my ignorance," Bob implored. "I've always been quartered with slaves and conflated my own situation with theirs. I'm trying to escape from a man who would enslave me for the rest of my life. He feels he has ownership of me because he paid my mother a large sum of money. He will keep me locked up and has threatened to beat me repeatedly until I willingly give in to his demands. If he captures me, I will never be free."

"Let me ask you sir. Did you come to this country kidnapped from your home and family, shackled to dozens of strangers, many of whom died around you, in the hold of a dark dank ship for six weeks, forced to lie on your back, unable to move in a stifling dark pit, nearly drowning in the urine and feces of everyone lying above and around you?

"No," Bob said quietly.

Do you have deep scars crisscrossing your back from being tied to a tree and beaten with a whip tied on the ends with rusty nails designed to rip the flesh off your back only to have salt poured into your wounds to prevent them from healing?

"No," he whispered.

Do you have a brand on your arm, back or face declaring who owns you?"

Bob's throat tightened. He wanted to speak, to protest, but nothing came. The weight of her words crushed the air from his lungs

Phillis' tone and anger rose higher with each declaration.

"Have your feet been deliberately broken to prevent you from running away? Have you been starved to the point that you pick garbage from the swill of pigs just to have something to eat? Has your hair been yanked from your head so violently that it ripped holes in your scalp exposing your brain tissue because you were too slow while picking cotton? Have your fingernails been pulled out one by one just to remind you who is boss? Have you been beaten nearly to death and several bones broken because you glanced at a white woman? Are there men with guns hunting you with dogs trained to tear you apart?"

Bob swallowed hard. He stared at the ground and shook his head. "No," he whispered.

"That is the life of a slave. Your problem is merely one of disappointment of how your life has gone so far. A white man always has choices; a slave never does. Good day to you sir." Phillis turned and walked away.

Bob slumped beneath the great elm, overwhelmed by shame and sorrow. He wept into his hands until exhaustion overcame him and sleep took him in its quiet mercy.

CHAPTER 8

The Green Dragon

MAY 6, 1782 – 10:00 A.M.

A sharp jab to his ribs shattered Bob's peaceful slumber.

"Please stop," implored Bob.

"At least you're alive," came a deep voice above him.

Bob cracked open one eye and squinted up into a halo of crimson. Standing over him was a tall man, well over six feet, dressed in a blood-red coat and looking like a scarlet specter. His cane hovered in the air, ready for another prod.

"You'd best get up, young man," the stranger said, scanning the Common. "If the constable catches you sleeping here, you'll spend a week in jail."

Bob yawned, rubbing the sleep from his eyes. "Thank you, sir. I didn't mean to break the law. I've been walking for two days, no food, no sleep. I didn't know it was illegal to sleep on the Common."

"What's your name, son?"

"Bob Shurtlieff."

"Well then, Bob Shurtlieff, do you have someplace to go?"

"A friend of mine, Toby Granger, told me to find the Green Dragon Tavern when I got to Boston. Said there'd be people there who could help me."

The man's eyes gleamed with surprise. "Toby, eh? I haven't seen him in years. Saved your life, did he?"

"Yes. I was being chased by some men trying to take me onto their ship. Toby popped right out of the ground like a rabbit. He helped me escape into a hidden cave covered in ancient paintings of animals that seemed to come alive when touched by torch light. He said the cave was sacred ground."

"That sounds exactly like Toby," the man said with a wide grin. "Name's Sam Adams. I'm headed to the Green Dragon myself to meet Paul Revere and Governor John Hancock. Why don't you join us? I'd wager they'd love to hear your story."

"Oh my. You, Paul, and John are who Toby said I should look for. How extraordinary that we should meet like this here on the Common!" exclaimed Bob.

"Sounds like Providence to me. I reckon this will prove to be a most entertaining meeting," said Sam, as he motioned for them to go.

They reached the tavern quickly. The upper floors housed the Freemasons of St. Andrew's Lodge, but the tavern itself lay in the cellar — a place where talk flowed as freely as cider and the business of revolution was conducted in guarded tones.

Above the narrow doorway swung a hammered-metal dragon on an iron bracket, its tongue jutting out in menace, teeth bared in frozen fury. Its wings raised as if ready to spring, its deep-green eyes gleamed with an almost living watchfulness, as though standing guard over all who entered.

Bob chuckled at the sight.

"What's so amusing?" Sam asked as they stepped inside.

"I once read that green dragons symbolize wisdom, power, and the beauty of nature," Bob replied.

"How fitting," Sam said. "That very dragon guards the door to the place where the Revolution was plotted. And now — thank God — we've nearly won."

Sam led Bob down a narrow staircase into the cellar. The ceiling was low, beams blackened by years of smoke; stone walls held the damp cool of the earth. At a table near the back sat Paul Revere and Governor John Hancock.

"Good morning, gentlemen," Sam said, gesturing to each. "Paul Revere. Governor John Hancock. May I introduce Bob Shurtlieff, a weary traveler just arrived this morning. He's a friend of Toby Granger."

Sam pulled out a chair. "Bob was just telling me what he's read about the symbolism of the Green Dragon."

Bob smiled, a little bashful.

"I've always had a taste for a good emblem," Revere said, his voice brisk and practical. "Symbols rally men faster than any shouted order."

"Quite so," Hancock agreed, setting down his coffee with measured grace. "And the dragon is a noble guardian — a fitting sentinel for liberty's cause."

"The dragon above the door represents wisdom, power, and the determination to protect what's worth defending," Bob said. "It reminded me of Thomas Paine's Common Sense."

"How so, old chap?" came a voice from behind.

They turned to see Thomas Paine, a half-smile on his lips. He joined them without ceremony.

"Tom! Perfect timing. This is Bob Shurtlieff," said Sam.

Bob rose and shook Paine's hand. "It's a great honor to meet you, sir."

"The pleasure's mine," Paine said, eyes bright. "Now — dragons and pamphlets? That's a pairing I'd like to hear explained."

"A dragon never surrenders," Bob said. "It fights to the last breath. That's what your words did — breathed fire into the will of a nation."

Paine's smile sharpened. "And how does our watchful friend outside tie to Common Sense?"

"You wrote, 'The cause of America is the cause of all mankind.' Like the dragon, your words refused to bow. They roused people to rise."

Revere tapped the table. "Once they had that courage, the rest was craft, planning, coordination, and striking at the right moment."

56

"Binding the colonies into one voice," Hancock added with pride. "A chorus so resolute it could not be ignored."

"Enough to stand against the mightiest empire in the world," Revere said.

Paine leaned back, satisfied. "Then perhaps the dragon has already done its work, not with teeth and claws, but with pen and paper. And I'd wager Washington has a bit of dragon in him too, never yielding, even when the lair was under siege."

Laughter circled the table. Conversation flowed on, with talk of symbols, liberty's stubborn fire, and the unity the fledgling nation would need. Bob listened, offered his thoughts when asked, and felt the weight of the company he kept.

Beneath the dragon's watchful eye, Bob understood that the creature they spoke of was not carved in metal above the door but lived in the hearts of those at this table.

"I really must be going," said John Hancock. "My brother Ebenezer is waiting for me to join him for dinner at his house next door. Bob. It was a pleasure to meet you. Hopefully, we can all meet again. I'd very much like to hear about your adventure with Toby."

"I am not sure how long I will be here," said Bob. "I'm hoping to join Washington's army."

"You're in luck, he's sent out a request for another 1500 soldiers. Sam and Paul can fill you in on the details," said John.

"That's great news, indeed. Thank you, sir," replied Bob.

"I hope you find the life and adventure you seek," said John.

Astonished, Bob smiled, "That's exactly what Toby said to me."

As John Hancock turned to walk away, Thomas said, "I'll walk with you, John. There's something I wish to discuss with you."

"Of course," said John.

"I bid you good day gentlemen," said Thomas. "It was a pleasure to meet you Bob."

Bob arose from his seat and extended his hand to Thomas. "The pleasure was all mine, sir."

The two great men walked away as the discussion at the table continued.

"Even though Cornwallis and his entire army surrendered in the south, skirmishes among the Patriots and Loyalists have increased here in the northeast," said Paul.

"Washington believes the British are going to try to redraw the border between Canada and America. They want to keep New York and have direct access to Canada by way of the Hudson River," added Sam.

"That would surely cripple trade for our country," said Bob.

"And keep us dependent on the British for any goods coming into New York. We'd have to pay very high import duties for essential items and be completely at the mercy of the British," said Paul.

"In essence, though we won the war, the entire economy of America would be totally controlled by the British if they keep New York and access to the Hudson River," added Sam.

"How ironic, it would seem that after all these years of fighting and lives lost, the future of our new nation depends entirely on what happens in this unstable period between war and peace," interjected Bob.

"That's what concerns Washington and is the reason he has asked for 1500 more men. He's going to create an elite special force of Rangers to protect the boundaries in the northeast and prevent the British from changing the borders in their favor, and essentially for them, winning the war," said Sam.

"The afternoon is winding on and I must be getting back to work," said Paul. "Bob, have you some place to stay at the moment?" inquired Paul.

"No, sir. I have not," said Bob.

"My typesetter is currently unwell and I need help at my shop," said Paul. "There's a room at the back you could use as your lodgings. As you're so well-read, you'd be the ideal candidate to help me. It's only for a few days, but that should see you through getting with a speculator and joining the army."

"Each town pays a different bounty for recruits. I'll make some inquiries and find out which will give you the most money," said Sam.

"This is wonderful!" said Bob. "I can't thank you enough."

"It's settled then," said Paul. "We best be going."

As they left the tavern and walked towards Paul's shop, located a short walk from the pub at number 8 Union Street, Bob felt a mixture of excitement and nervousness about the future. He never imagined that he would meet four of the country's greatest leaders. These four men led the country to fight against the British and started the movement that became the Revolutionary War. The fact that Paul Revere and Sam Adams were willing to help him join Washington's army, and to support the fight for independence, filled Bob with purpose and determination. Paul's offer of a temporary place to stay and work was a turning point in Bob's journey.

Bob was a quick learner. He quickly settled into his temporary lodgings and immersed himself in the work, eager to contribute and learn from the experienced printer. The most difficult part of the job was spelling everything backwards, so it would appear the right way around when printed. The rhythmic clatter of the printing press filled the room; a constant reminder of the important role Paul Revere played in disseminating information crucial to the revolutionary cause.

Five days later, Sam sent word to Paul that he had the information Bob needed to get the highest bounty for joining the army. They agreed to meet for lunch the next day at the Green Dragon.

Bob and Paul arrived at noon and seated themselves at the same table at the back of the room where they'd sat before.

"Is this the same table where you and the others were sitting when you started preparing for the war?" asked Bob with a grin.

"Yes. This is the table we still use for the planning committee. The waiters know our routine and keep it clear for us," said Paul.

Bob looked at Paul and smiled. "Perhaps one day I shall return to this very spot and find a brass plaque hammered into this table that reads, Sam Adams, Paul Revere, John Hancock and Thomas Paine sat at this table to plan the Revolutionary War."

The tavern was bustling as Sam, in his dark red suit, made his way through the crowd to join them. "Hello, chaps."

"Hi Sam," said Bob.

"What's the news?" asked Paul.

"It seems that Uxbridge is offering sixty pounds for new recruits," replied Sam.

"I never imagined it would be such a princely sum!" exclaimed Bob.

"How long is the term of enlistment?" asked Paul.

"Three years," replied Sam.

"That explains why they're paying so much money," said Paul.

"The recruiter is currently in Bellingham. His name is Noah Taft," said Sam.

"How far away is that from Boston?" asked Bob.

"Forty miles," said Sam.

"When will you be leaving?" asked Paul.

"When do you expect your typesetter to be back to work?" asked Bob.

"He's coming back tomorrow," said Paul.

"Then I'll leave tomorrow," replied Bob.

"Now that's settled, let's have lunch," said Sam. "I'm starving."

The next morning, a warm orange glow from the sun poured through the windows, lighting up Paul's shop. Bob had gotten up early and got the press ready, swept out the shop and was waiting for Paul to arrive.

"Good morning Bob," said Paul. "I see you're ready to go."

"I thought it best to get started as soon as possible," said Bob.

Paul handed Bob a small bundle tied with string. "Rachel put together some food for your trip."

"That's very kind. Please thank her for me," replied Bob.

Paul reached into his pocket and pulled out five shillings and handed them to Bob. "Here, this should see you through till you join the army."

Bob was astonished. "You gave me free room and board. I wasn't expecting to get paid as well."

"You're an excellent worker and I'm grateful for your help," answered Paul.

"I can't thank you enough for everything," said Bob. "I hope one day I can repay your kindness."

"When you get to West Point, you'd do well to get into Captain George Webb's company. He is a friend of mine and his light infantry company is a new elite unit of soldiers called Rangers. He has some very specific requirements for soldiers wanting to join his company and you certainly meet all of them. That's where you want to be assigned. Tell him you're there on my recommendation," said Paul.

"Thank you so much for the reference to Captain Webb. I'll be sure to write and let you know if I get accepted."

"Remember, be the best soldier you can be and serve our country with honor and valor," said Paul.

"I promise I will do my best to make you and Sam proud," said Bob with tears in his eyes as he turned to leave.

With a grateful heart and a newfound purpose, Bob stepped into the morning light, bound for Bellingham.

The road ahead was long, the way uncertain. The same flame that once ignited a revolution now burned in him. He would carry that flame forward, not as a runaway or a servant, but as a Ranger, a soldier, a free man.

CHAPTER 9

The Speculator

MAY 20, 1782

The Stag's Head pub stood at the heart of Bellingham, its beams leaning slightly with age, yet proud. Bob pushed through the heavy oak door and stepped into the tavern's warm hearth-glow.

Laughter mingled with the scent of roasting meat, woodsmoke, and cider. Bob's stomach groaned. He hadn't eaten since dawn.

A stout man, red-faced and harried, burst from the crowd and nearly knocked him over.

"Pardon, lad, urgent business," the man grunted.

Bob froze. It was Simon Alden, a Baptist elder. Two months before, Alden had been a guest preacher at the Third Baptist Church in Middleborough, filling in for Pastor Allen, who was on a trip to visit relatives in New York.

Alden preached a sermon saying that no man or woman can hide behind falsehood and walk freely in the Light of God. His words sliced through Deborah, now disguised as Bob Shurtlieff, like scripture turned into a sword. Afterall, that's exactly what she had been planning to do. She'd sat directly in front of the pulpit, Alden's gaze like a judgment. He looked at her often, as if he were seeing into her soul, knowing she was about to sin.

Fighting back the instinct to run away, Bob found an empty seat by the fire to wait and see what would happen.

Alden soon returned, his expression transformed into something almost paternal. "May I join you?"

A firm handshake followed. "Simon Alden. Apologies for the earlier commotion."

"Bob Shurtlieff," he replied. "No harm done."

Alden squinted. "You look familiar. Have we met?"

"I don't believe so," Bob said carefully.

Lowering his voice, Alden asked, "I'm collecting for war widows and orphans. Care to help?"

"I'm afraid I've barely got enough to get to West Point, where I'm hoping to join the army," Bob answered honestly.

Alden nodded. "Then you're in luck. That's Noah Taft at the bar. He's a speculator recruiting able-bodied men for the army and paying them a hefty bounty to enlist. Right now, he's working for the town of Uxbridge to fill their quota, replacements for those unwilling to serve. Might be just what you're looking for."

Bob followed Alden's gaze to a hulking man nursing a pint of cider, the very man he'd just traveled 40 miles to meet.

"Good evening, sir. My name is Bob Shurtlieff."

"Noah Taft," he said, extending his hand. "You want to join the army?"

"Yes, I do." Bob stood taller. "As Thomas Paine said, 'The sun never shined on a cause of greater worth.' I want to fight for liberty, sir."

Taft grunted approval. "You'll be paid a $60 bonus for a three-year enlistment. Agreed?"

"Yes, sir."

Taft opened his ledger. Most names were marked with an X. Bob signed his name, Robert Shurtlieff, slowly and deliberately.

"A literate man, eh? That'll serve you well in the army," Noah said.

Bob grinned. "I was a teacher."

"Meet me here at 8:00 a.m.," Taft said. "We'll head to Worcester for muster and swearing-in."

Bob beamed with pride as he returned to the table. He felt a sense of purpose had come into his life.

Alden clapped him on the back as he got up to leave. "Well done, boy!"

With Alden gone, Bob collapsed back in his chair, relief washing over him. His disguise had worked.

The barmaid drifted over to Bob's table, her Irish lilt soft and friendly. "What'll you be having tonight, sir?"

"A pint of cider, whatever's on the fire—and a bed for the night," Bob said.

She smiled. "Roast beef and potatoes, if that suits. As for the bed, there's but one left upstairs. You'll have it."

Bob nodded. "Thank you."

While waiting for his meal, Bob watched Simon Alden as he made his way around the room asking for donations. He wondered if any of that money ever made it to the widows and orphans?

Within a matter of minutes, the barmaid returned with his food and drink. A sense of relief at not being discovered washed over Bob.

After finishing his meal, Bob went up the stairs to his room. It had six beds and was far better than the last place that had nothing but straw mats on the floor. Bob whispered a prayer of thanks and fell fast asleep, until the nightmare began.

In a fog-shrouded sea, a bell was ringing. Then, a pirate ship appeared. Screaming men swung aboard. It was Beecham, his face aflame as he raised his blade.

"Welcome to hell. You can't escape me, boy. I know your sins."

Bob thrashed in bed, then screamed.

"Wake up, boy! You're dreaming," said a man in the next bed.

Bob bolted upright.

"So sorry. I didn't mean to wake you," said Bob, gasping for breath.

"Sounded terrible," said the man.

"It was, pirates. One of them was a man named Beecham. He tried to Shanghai me."

"You knew him?"

Bob nodded. "I escaped. But I'm still afraid he might find me one day and force me onto his ship."

"I understand," said the sailor. "We too were attacked once by pirates. I'm lucky to be alive."

They talked for awhile, until Bob's nerves had calmed down from the nightmare. The sailor said he was headed to Plymouth to work on a ship taking slaves to the West Indies.

"It's a death sentence," he muttered. "They'll be gone within the year."

"Then maybe heaven will greet them with mercy," said Bob quietly.

"True enough. Well, I'll say goodnight then. Let's hope you can get some sleep," said the man.

"Thank you, I'll try," sighed Bob.

Bob struggled for hours to get the terrifying images of his dream out of his mind. He finally fell asleep, only to be awakened just before dawn by the men in the other beds getting up and jostling to use the chamber pot before moving on. It was 6:00 a.m. and he wasn't meeting with Noah Taft until 8:00 a.m. The acrid smell of urine made Bob nauseous. *Might as well get up*, he thought.

Bob knelt next to his bed in the now empty room. He silently pleaded with God to forgive his sins and to help him to pass muster and join the Continental Army. If his secret were somehow revealed during the muster, the consequences could mean a public beating and possibly even jail.

Heading down the stairs, Bob's mouth watered as he inhaled the aroma of hot coffee and freshly baked bread that filled the pub. He was surprised to see Noah Taft already sitting at a table with two men, who looked considerably older than Bob. "Pull up a chair, boy."

Bob shook hands with the two men. "Bob Shurtlieff."

"Richard Snow."

"Dale Lally."

"Nice to meet you both."

They shared breakfast, then climbed into Taft's wagon for the two-day trip to Worcester, bouncing along rutted roads seated on bales of hay.

They finally arrived in the evening as the clock tower, located in the heart of Worcester, chimed seven times. Bob's tension had eased slightly during the trip. After all, he had just spent two days in close proximity to three men who had no clue as to Bob's true identity. His years as an indentured servant, looking after the sons of the Reverend Thomas, taught him a great deal about how to talk and act around men. All was going to plan, or so he thought.

Taft strode up to the campfire which was surrounded by seasoned soldiers, whose composure exuded a sense of discipline and purpose. Their weathered uniforms serving as a testament to the harsh realities of war.

"Evening, Sergeant Munn. Here's three more recruits."

Sergeant Munn eyed them with suspicion, then motioned for the men to come closer.

"These three look fit enough — not like the sorry dregs you shoved at us before."

Taft shrugged. "It's slim pickin's these days."

"Alright men, go draw your rations. Then find a tent and get some sleep. You'll be called to muster at 7:00 a.m."

There wasn't much food when they got to the mess fire. About three cups of what was a sorry excuse for a stew was all that was left in the pot. They portioned it out equally and were grateful to have anything at all.

As they walked through the camp, Bob was stunned to see that most of the fifty or so recruits were teenagers. Some he guessed were as young as eight years old.

The only unoccupied tents left were at the back of the camp near the latrines. The stench was overwhelming.

"I'm not sleeping here," said Richard.

"It's disgusting," said Dale.

"Let's see if we can find a tent near the front we can squeeze into," said Bob.

The men headed back near the front and found boys who were scared and homesick, willing to let them share their tents.

Bob was awake and saying his morning prayers, long before the drums sounded the wake-up signal at 6:30 a.m., stirring the camp to life. Soon, the fifty or so recruits were all standing at the front of the camp, waiting.

"Sergeant Munn, call the men to order," said Captain Eliphalet Thorpe, the muster master in charge of the camp.

"Yes, Captain." Turning to the men, Munn shouted, "Form a line according to height, the shortest at this end, the tallest at that end. No talking."

Bob, Dale, and Richard took up their position at the far end. They were by far the tallest and oldest recruits. Standing at 5'10", Bob was the last in line.

The young recruits scrambled to find their places. Most of the boys wore clothes that were pockmarked with holes. Ropes tied at the waist held up what was left of their ragged breeches. Their bare feet kicked up clouds of dust that quickly settled like fine ashes on their threadbare clothes.

Many of the boys were orphans, having lost their fathers to the war. Bob looked with pity on this motley group. He knew their lives depended on getting into the Army. At least they wouldn't starve and would get uniforms to replace their rags.

Captain Thorpe was responsible for the arduous task of ensuring the regiment's ranks were filled with able-bodied men. With a keen eye for detail, and an unwavering dedication to his duties, Thorpe meticulously reviewed each recruit, verifying their identities and determining if a recruit was fit for duty.

As Thorpe passed down the line, Bob watched as each of the boys stood as tall as possible. One of the boys, who was about twelve years old, started to cough uncontrollably.

"Name and where you're from," Thorpe said.

Barely able to speak, the boy rasped, "Michael Evans from Paxton, sir."

The boy held his hand over his mouth, desperately trying not to cough, which only made it worse. As Thorpe stepped in front of the boy, his cough was like a volcanic eruption. Blood splattered through the boy's fingers, landing squarely across the chest of Captain Thorpe.

"Sergeant Munn, this young man is clearly not fit to serve. Send him to the surgeon's tent and then back to wherever he came from."

The boy collapsed at Thorpe's feet, sputtering breathlessly. "Please sir, my family are all dead. I have no place to go back to."

Wiping the blood off his uniform with his handkerchief, the Captain shouted, "Now, Munn, before we all get sick from whatever his affliction is."

Munn grabbed the boy by his shirt and began to drag him away. The boy stumbled desperately trying to get on his feet. Munn shouted, "Get up, you mangy dog."

Bob's instincts took over. He ran forward. "Let me help him, Sergeant. I'll see him to the surgeon's tent."

Munn let go of the boy and glared at Bob. "Take him, then. And don't bother coming back."

CHAPTER 10

Latrine Duty

MAY 23, 1782

The sergeant's words struck Bob like a musket ball to the gut. Stepping forward to help that fever-struck boy had not been a choice, it was a reflex, bred into his very bones. But now, as each recruit shuffled forward, under Captain Thorpe's scrutiny, it felt as though the future Bob had fought for, walked for, prayed for, was melting away like snow under the sun.

The boy, Michael Evans, ghostly pale and drenched in sweat, shook his head at Bob as he stumbled away. He had the same hollow eyes and waxen skin as Mr. Graham, the dream-reader from Middleborough who'd declared Bob's nightmare a good omen. It was the look of someone slipping away from this life and into the next.

Bob watched the boy go, then silently took his place back at the end of the line.

Captain Thorpe, compact and stern, continued down the line, inspecting each recruit like livestock before market. Dale Lally passed muster with ease, grinning like a man already drunk on victory. Richard Snow followed, his lanky frame swaying in place with nervous energy.

Then, the Captain stopped in front of Bob.

He had to crane his neck to look up. Bob stood nearly a head taller; the steel in Thorpe's gaze didn't waver.

"Name and where you're from?"

"Bob Shurtlieff from Carver, Massachusetts, sir."

Thorpe narrowed his eyes. "You've already demonstrated a fondness for ignoring orders. Why, precisely, should I let you into the Continental army?"

Bob cleared his throat, summoning all the confidence he could muster.

"I've done as I was bid since I was five, sir. Served my masters well — never a complaint. As for soldiering: I can shoot the eye out of a squirrel at twenty feet, break and ride the meanest horse in the field, and outrun most men. I can read and write, too, and taught school three years."

A flicker of something, approval perhaps, passed across Thorpe's face. "Let's hope you use those talents well, Shurtlieff."

"Thank you, sir. I won't disappoint you."

"Sergeant Munn," the Captain barked. "Begin to break camp. We march for West Point at first light."

"Yes, sir!"

The weight of dread lifted from Bob's chest, as if a chain had dropped away. He turned skyward and prayed silently. *Thank You, Lord, for this blessing, not only for me, but also for the others. May I prove worthy of this new life You've given me.*

Richard clapped him on the back. "You had us worried, Shurtlieff. What were you thinking?"

"I couldn't watch that boy suffer," Bob admitted. "I had to do something."

Richard and Dale shook their heads in disbelief.

"You almost threw your life away with his," said Dale.

"Not really. I trust in the Lord. If I do what's right by Him, He'll do right by me."

Dale raised a brow. "Let's hope your Lord keeps His end of the bargain."

"He always has."

Richard grinned. "Let's go get our bounty."

At the quartermaster's tent, Bob signed his name with care and pocketed the hard silver of his enlistment bounty.

Holding up his receipt, Bob beamed as he read: "Recruit of Mr. Noah Taft, Chairman of Class No. 2, sons of Uxbridge. Dated May 23rd, 1782. Sum of sixty pounds. Term: three years."

"Hallelujah! I'm in the army now! West Point, here I come!" shouted Bob.

Later that afternoon, Sergeant Munn called the recruits to order. "Listen up! The war's nearly done, and you're the last batch of recruits to come through this camp. We're going to break everything down and load it all onto the wagons.

You'll be split into teams. Each team will have a leader and an assigned task. Any questions, ask your leader."

In mid-afternoon, Bob slipped away to relieve himself. He walked deep into the woods, past the stench of the camp latrines, to a quiet glade. As he squatted behind a thicket, a faint gurgling caught his ear.

Ten feet away, hidden by an old fallen tree, lay Michael Evans, his body limp, lips bloodied.

Bob dropped beside him, pulling the frail body into his arms.

"You're free to go now," he whispered. "No more suffering."

Michael's eyes opened for a final moment. His mouth formed a faint smile as he exhaled his last breath.

Bob dug the grave himself, fast and deep, tears smearing the dirt on his cheeks. He laid the boy to rest, covered him with stones, and marked the spot with a crude cross made of branches.

Kneeling, he prayed, "Lord, grant Michael Your peace. Let him be seen, known, and loved in Your kingdom, where sorrow does not dwell."

Back in camp, Dale and Richard were packing supplies onto the wagon.

"Where were you?" Dale asked. "Munn's been asking."

"I found the boy. He died in my arms."

"At least he wasn't alone," said Richard.

"What'd you do with the body?"

"I buried him."

Richard scoffed. "Your God didn't help him."

Bob shook his head. "The Lord may not spare us the pain, but He never leaves us to suffer it alone."

Sergeant Munn spotted him. "Shurtlieff! Over here."

"Yes, Sergeant."

"Where've you been?"

"Relieving myself, sir."

"For an hour?"

"I found Michael Evans, dead in the brush, so I buried him."

"Well, since you like digging so much, go bury the latrines, every pit. Don't stop until they're all filled in."

"Yes, Sergeant."

The stench of years clung to the latrine fields, an acre of filth and disease. Rain had turned the muck into rivers. Flies swarmed. Bob tied his handkerchief around his face and began.

As he shoveled, Richard wandered over. "Looks like your God's punishing you."

"You sound like Job's friends," Bob replied.

"Why'd God let Satan test him, then?"

"To prove that true faith endures."

Richard looked down at the mud. "Let's hope yours does."

At dinnertime, everyone but Bob moved toward the cook fires

Dale lingered. "I admire your faith, Bob. I'd like to learn more if you'll teach me."

Bob smiled. "Whenever you're ready."

It was after midnight when Sgt. Munn sent Private Orrick to check Bob's progress. He reported that only one pit remained to be filled in.

Near two in the morning, Bob returned to camp, pulling a crust of bread from his pocket that Dale had given to him. Just as he raised it to his lips, Sergeant Munn appeared.

"Where'd you get that food, boy?"

"I haven't eaten in fourteen hours, Sergeant. A kind soul offered me this, and I saved it until now. Am I to be punished for accepting kindness?"

Munn's eyes narrowed, then rolled. "Get to bed, Shurtlieff."

"Yes, Sergeant."

He lay down at last, back sore, belly aching, heart full. Surely, he thought, it can only get better from here.

Bob was dreaming. An enormous sea monster, a Leviathan, surged up from the deep, its teeth glinting like steel in the murk. The beast's eyes glowed like burning coal—a judgment, or a warning—he couldn't tell. He fought it with all his might, muscles straining, heart pounding, until a jarring shake tore him from the fray.

"Wake up, man!" Dale said. "Sergeant Munn's called muster. If you don't move your arse, you'll feel his wrath soon enough."

Bob jerked upright, a gasp catching in his throat as his arms flailed instinctively, warding off the phantom beast. It took a moment for the fog of sleep to clear, his eyes adjusting to the dim light of the tent.

Outside, the camp was already in motion. The sole remaining latrine was ringed with men of all sizes and ranks, a chaotic scene of necessity that left Bob grimacing. He slipped away, seeking the relative privacy of the woods to relieve himself before returning to grab his ration of breakfast, gruel, bland and unremarkable, but enough to stoke his energy for the tasks ahead.

By the time the company fell into line to march, Bob had finished filling in the last latrine trench, a task that left his muscles aching but his mind oddly at ease. He paused for a moment in the clearing, now eerily empty. Six years of war had carved its stories into this soil, and now, as the army prepared to move on, Bob felt both the weight and the wonder of it.

He bent his head, murmuring a prayer of thanks for the small role he was about to play in this vast endeavor. *What an extraordinary thing,* he thought, *for farmers and tradesmen, boys, and seasoned men alike, to rise against the greatest empire of their age. To fight, not for a king's command, but for a dream—and win!*

CHAPTER 11

Lynchpin Of The War

MAY 27, 1782

The march to West Point took several days through forests that pressed close on either side, the towering trees casting shadows across the narrow trail. When they finally reached the Hudson, its broad expanse gleamed under the noonday sun. Bob felt a pang of awe.

The river flowed with an almost holy grandeur, its banks fringed with cliffs draped in verdant green. The fortifications atop those cliffs loomed like sentinels, their battered walls bearing witness to the brutal chess game of war.

At Kings Ferry, the troops began crossing in groups. Bob was assigned to the last group, leaving him with a couple of hours to spare. Lost in thought, he strayed farther than he realized. When at last he emerged from the woods, his stomach plunged. The final ferry was shoving off; the troops were already aboard.

"No! Wait!" he shouted, breaking into a sprint.

The slope down to the beach was steep and unforgiving. Halfway down, his foot caught on a loose stone, sending him tumbling in a graceless sprawl. He hit the beach with a jarring thud but scrambled to his feet, adrenaline overriding pain. The ferry was pulling away, and with a desperate burst of speed, he leapt—and caught the edge of the ferry with both hands.

The impact sent a shudder through the craft, nearly unseating Sergeant Munn himself. He spun around, his face a mask of fury as Bob clambered aboard with the help of Dale and Richard.

"Shurtlieff!" Munn roared. "You could've drowned us all with that stunt! What were you thinking?"

Bob stood panting, water dripping from his uniform, but he met the sergeant's glare with steady resolve.

"Apologies, Sergeant. I didn't want to be left behind."

"Then you should've stayed where you bloody belonged!"

The tension hung thick, but Bob seized the moment to redirect. "Sergeant, this place... it's the lynchpin of the war, isn't it? If the British take control of the Hudson, they'll strangle us economically and divide us politically."

Munn's anger faltered, replaced by a begrudging nod. "Aye. Washington keeps his eyes on this place like a hawk."

Minutes later, Bob stepped off the ferry onto the muddy bank, his shoes sinking slightly into the earth. The weight of the place settled over him, the grandeur of the landscape, the grim determination of the men who fought to defend it and the quiet, persistent hum of hope threading through it all. It was a land caught between war and peace, beauty and brutality, wildness and order. And it was alive.

Sergeant Munn led the way up the narrow twisting trail, with the last of the new recruits following behind him. They were like a gaggle of squawking geese, filled with a combination of awe and excitement.

West Point rose from the earth, as though it had grown there. A sprawling mass of stone walls and timbered barracks perched on the edge of the river. Cannon muzzles jutted from the parapets, their dark barrels glinting ominously in the afternoon light.

Below, Washington's Great Chain stretched across the Hudson. The immense barrier was made up of eighteen tons of forged iron, held together by 850 individual iron links, each weighing one hundred and forty pounds. Anchored to both shores, it was a bold declaration: the Hudson River would not be ceded to the British without a fight. Each link lay heavy in the water, a silent promise of defiance.

Walking through the gate at West Point, Bob could see the fort was alive with purpose. Soldiers milled about, their movements resolute, their voices edged with determination and fatigue. Bob recognized a young boy, who was no older than fourteen, and one of his own group of recruits, scurry past, his arms loaded with a pile of muskets nearly as tall as he was. Bob sidestepped him and pressed on, his gaze sweeping the expanse. Here was the beating heart of the revolution. Not the glory-laden battlefields where generals made speeches, but this, the grim, practical work of survival, resistance, and defense.

"Private Orrick, muster the men on the parade field," said Sgt. Munn.

"Yes, Sergeant," replied Orrick.

The recruits who'd arrived hours before Bob, were huddled together on the ground looking exhausted. They'd been working to shift all the supplies that had come from the camp at Worcester, up the steep trail from the water's edge to the storage area, near the fort's stone walls on the far side of the parade grounds.

Orrick shouted at the group. "Time to muster."

They all jumped up like a mob of meerkats and ran with Orrick to the wide open field. It served as the lungs of the fortress, inhaling the chaos of daily life and exhaling the discipline of an army.

Bordered by the rugged walls of the fort, the field extended all the way up to the deep, green expanse of the surrounding forest. Its edges blending unevenly into the hills and cliffs that tumbled toward the river. This was a space alive with purpose, the kind of place where a thousand things seemed to happen at once, all overlapping in a symphony of noise, movement, and grit.

To one side of the field, tents were pitched in neat rows, their white canvas stained with soot and mud, flapping lazily in the breeze. Smoke curled from campfires scattered among them. The scent of charred wood mingled with the earthy tang of cooking meat and the faint, sharp edge of unwashed bodies. Soldiers crouched around the fires. Their faces, lined with fatigue, as they ladled thin stew into battered tin bowls, grateful to have something to eat.

The center of the field served as the parade ground, a space reserved for ceremony and punishment alike. It was here that victories were celebrated, green recruits became hardened soldiers, and deserters were flogged, a grim counterpoint to the formalities of military life. Everything about the space was both utilitarian and alive, as though the field itself was a living, breathing thing.

Bob chuckled to himself as he saw a group of boys, too young for battle, practicing their drills with sticks and wooden swords, their laughter rising above the din of the camp.

"Line up in five rows of ten men each from left to right, shortest to the tallest, and stand at attention," said Orrick.

In double-quick time the recruits got into formation, as they had learned this at the camp in Worcester. Bob was last in line, next to Dale and Richard.

Sergeant Munn stood before them, his voice cutting through the air like a whip. "You call that standing at attention?" he bellowed, pacing slowly along the line.

His eyes flicked from one man to the next, pausing just long enough to make each recruit feel the weight of his scrutiny.

"You're soldiers of the Continental Army now, not a pack of farmers fresh off the plow! Shoulders back, chin up, chest out."

Captain Thorpe came to inspect the troops, accompanied by Captain George Webb, an officer in the prestigious Light Infantry Company of the Fourth Massachusetts Regiment. As they walked along the line, Sergeant Munn followed behind them. The first in line, and the shortest boy in group, Roger

Barrett, was the same boy that Bob saw earlier carrying the load of muskets. The inspection began with him.

"What's your name and how old are you?" asked Webb.

"Roger Barrett, age 14, sir."

"Why have you joined the army?" asked Thorpe.

"My family was all murdered, sir," Barrett replied.

"Who killed them?" asked Webb.

"Colonel James Delancey, the Sheriff of Westchester County and his raiders," Barrett replied.

"Why did he kill your family?" asked Webb.

"Because we're Patriots. He said we had to leave Westchester. It was his county and only Loyalists were allowed to live there."

Thorpe's voice lowered. "Then what happened?"

"My Pa told him we weren't going anywhere and the only way he'd get us to leave was to kill us," said Roger. "Delancey pulled out a pistol and shot my father in the head. Mother and my sister started to scream. Two other men pulled out their pistols and shot them in the head as well. Delancey told his men to drag the bodies into the cabin and burn it."

"How is it you weren't killed?" asked Webb.

"I was out in the woods checking my rabbit traps when I saw them coming. I ran fast as I could back to the house to warn them. But as I got closer, I could hear what they were saying, so I stayed hidden in the bushes. I saw everything. My father told me that if ever I saw something like that happening, I was to stay quiet and keep out of sight. It was really hard to do. So, after they killed my family, that's when

I decided I would join the army and maybe I'd get a chance to kill James Delancey and the other two men who shot my mother and sister."

"You'll be pleased to know that Delancey is at the top of General Washington's most wanted list," replied Webb. "Because you've actually seen Delancey, you could play a vital role when it comes to identifying him."

"I'll never forget his face, sir," said Roger. "It's the face of the devil himself."

The officers continued to inspect the troops. However, it was those who were the last in line, the tallest recruits, that Webb was interested in. To be in Webb's special forces, a soldier had to be at least five feet seven inches tall, highly intelligent, have a good disposition, and be courageous.

Webb stopped at Richard Snow. "What's your name?"

"Step forward when being addressed by the Captain," said Ensign Towne.

Standing tall and looking straight ahead, he nervously responded, "Richard Snow, sir."

"Where're you from?" asked Webb.

"Boston, sir."

"What did you do there?"

"I worked in a bookshop, until the owner died and his family sold the business, which put me out of a job."

"Why did you join the army?" asked Webb.

"I'd been reading Thomas Paine's *American Crisis* articles. He writes about how the war is still on-going and fresh troops are needed to insure the British are utterly defeated. I thought my organizational skills, along with my ability to read, write, and do math might be of service to the army and help us to cross the finish line to victory."

"Those are very noble sentiments, indeed," said Webb.

He moved onto Dale. "What is your name and where're you from?"

"My name is Dale Lally and I came to this country five years ago from Dublin, Ireland to work as an indentured servant for my father's brother, my uncle, Ken Lally. He had a sheep farm on the outskirts of Philadelphia."

"Why did you leave your uncle's employment?" asked Webb.

"Unfortunately, my uncle and his wife, Bertha, both died of scarlet fever, just days apart. My uncle treated me like a son and included me in family meetings about the business. He was appreciative of my knowledge and skill in managing the farm and had shown great respect for my suggestions on ways to increase and improve the livestock. His three sons were not interested in the family business, except for what they could get out of it.

He also taught me how to hunt, shoot, and process the prey quickly. I excelled at this as well, which only served to infuriate my cousins even more. My uncle told me he had left provisions for me in his will as payment for all I had done to increase his stock, which made him a very wealthy man. However, once he died, they lost no time in getting me out of the way. They said their father never left me anything, and if I ever came back, they'd have me arrested for trespassing."

"How did you end up here at West Point?" asked Webb.

"I was heading to Boston to find work and stopped at a pub in Bellingham, Massachusetts. That's where I met Noah Taft, the speculator from Uxbridge. He convinced me that the army was the best place for me, as I was a good hunter."

"You've made the right decision. Welcome to West Point and the Continental Army," said Webb.

Webb moved onto Bob.

"Tell me your name and where you're from."

Bob stepped forward and looked straight ahead. "Bob Shurtlieff, sir, from Carver Massachusetts."

"Tell me what brings you to West Point?" asked Webb.

"Well, sir, you do."

"Explain what you mean by that."

"We have a mutual friend, Paul Revere. Sam Adams introduced me to Paul, along with John Hancock and Thomas Paine at the Green Dragon pub in Boston. I worked with Paul for a brief time in Boston while his assistant was out sick. Paul knew I was planning to join the army and said I should go to West Point and apply to join your company. He said you've created a new crack unit of soldiers called Rangers that are being trained by Baron Von Steuben himself. Paul said he felt I met all the requirements to join your group."

Webb's eyes lit up and he smiled at Bob. "Well, young man, you certainly travel in prestigious company. You cannot get a better reference than from Paul Revere."

"Thank you, sir. I promised Paul, should you accept me into your company, I'll try my hardest to be the best Ranger possible."

"As long as you can pass the training, you'll be on your way to keeping that promise. Welcome to the Light Infantry," said Webb.

Overwhelmed by this miraculous turn of events, Bob said a silent prayer of gratitude.

Thank you so much Lord for getting me farther than I ever imagined possible and into this elite company, a Ranger no less! I promise, Lord, to do my best and to never let you down.

Webb turned to Ensign Towne. "See these three men properly outfitted and have them report to my company."

"Yes, Captain," Towne replied.

Thorpe and Webb turned and walked away. "Finally, we're getting some quality recruits," said Webb.

"Recommended by Paul Revere, no less!" said Thorpe. "Lally and Snow should do well. But we've had some problems with Shurtlieff along the way."

"What sort of problems?" asked Webb.

"I'll tell you over dinner. I'm famished," said Thorpe.

Bob, Richard, and Dale had been dismissed with curt instructions from Sergeant Munn to report to the commissary first thing in the morning, to be fitted for their new Ranger uniforms and supplies and then report to Webb's company to begin training.

"Light Infantry," Richard murmured, half to himself, his voice tinged with awe. "Never thought I'd be chosen for something like that."

Dale grinned, his eyes crinkling beneath the brim of his hat. "Guess Webb sees something of value in us. Best not to disappoint him."

Bob kept quiet, though his chest swelled with a mix of pride and trepidation. Every step brought him further into the life he had chosen. There was no turning back now.

CHAPTER 12

Rangers In Uniform

MAY 28, 1782

After breakfast at the cookhouse, Bob, Richard, and Dale headed to the commissary, a squat, weathered building made of rough-hewn timber. Its roof sagged slightly in the middle, and the windows were small and set high in the walls, but it was bustling with activity. Soldiers milled about, some leaving with bundles of supplies, others waiting to be seen.

Inside, the air was cooler but thick with the smell of wool, leather, and oiled metal. The man who oversaw the commissary, Africa Hamlin, was a study in contradictions. His honey-colored skin caught the warm glow of the morning sun, lending an almost golden hue to his rugged features. A thick, bushy beard framed his strong jaw, streaked faintly with silver that betrayed his years, though his sharp eyes missed nothing.

Hamlin stood with the unyielding posture of a man accustomed to command, his hands thick and calloused, moving with an efficiency born of years in the trade. A scowl seemed permanently etched onto his face, as though the very idea of smiling was beneath him. He barely looked up as the three men entered the room.

Bob couldn't help but notice the sheer presence of the man. His voice carried a gravelly weight that brooked no argument, and when he spoke, it was with the authority of someone who expected to be obeyed without question. Yet beneath the gruff exterior, there was an undeniable air of competence, a steadiness that reassured anyone who crossed his path that, whatever else might go wrong, the commissary would not.

"Names?" he barked.

"Richard Snow."

"Dale Lally."

"Bob Shurtlieff."

"Company?"

"We're all with Captain Webb's Light Infantry, Fourth Massachusetts Regiment," replied Bob.

"Light Infantry, huh?" His tone carried a note of skepticism as his eyes roved over them. "We'll see how long you last."

He gestured toward a rack of uniforms hanging in neat rows. "Try those on. Shoes are over there. Belts, cartridge boxes, knives, pistols, muskets, and bayonets at the end."

The uniforms were striking: a dark blue coat with short tails, its lapels and cuffs edged in white. The brass buttons gleamed, and the wool was coarse but sturdy, designed to withstand the rigors of a soldier's life. Beneath the coat, a sleeveless waistcoat of white wool hugged close over a plain linen shirt, loose at the neck, its ties hanging undone beneath the stock. The shirt served a dual purpose worn by day beneath the coat and waistcoat, and to cover the body at night.

Below that, snug white breeches fastened at the knee with black straps, paired with black gaiters that buckled down tight over square-toed leather shoes.

Atop it all, the cap. Made of black leather, close-fitting, with a brass badge in the shape of a hunting horn, the mark of light infantry, and a black cockade pinned to the side.

Bob ran his fingers over the coat's fabric, the weight of it grounding him. This wasn't just clothing; it was a symbol of his commitment, his disguise, his protection.

They took turns changing behind a wooden partition. Bob insisted on going last, using the extra time to mentally prepare. When it was his turn, he slipped behind the screen, his heart pounding.

By the time he stepped out, the others were waiting, their own uniforms slightly rumpled but giving them an air of pride.

"Not bad," Richard said, grinning as he tightened his belt. "We look like real soldiers now."

"Yeah," Bob murmured, adjusting his cap. "Real soldiers."

"The uniforms all come in standard sizes. We can alter them right here," Hamlin said. "Snow, your uniform will need to be adjusted in the shoulders and the waist. Stand here while I take some measurements."

Snow stepped forward. Bob watched as Hamlin's hands pressed down on Snow's chest as he stretched his paper tape with markings for a half-measure going from Snow's sternum to his spine.

"The coat will need to be taken in, but not by much, just a couple of inches." Then Hamlin pulled up on Snow's breeches, causing his manhood to bulge uncomfortably beneath the coarse fabric. "These too, will need to be trimmed down."

"How long will that take? We have to report in uniform today," said Snow.

"Fortunately, there are several women in camp who do quick alterations. They work in teams and are very fast."

"Where do I find the women?" asked Snow.

"Many of the soldiers have their families here with them. Their camp is on the north side of the parade ground. You can't miss it. Those women are what keep West Point running smoothly doing the laundry, sewing, and cooking for the soldiers. Most of these soldiers couldn't manage without them."

"Anyone in particular I should ask for," asked Snow.

"Yes. Sarah Osborn. She should be able to get you fitted today," said Hamlin.

"Thank you. I'll go there now," said Snow.

"Okay. Who's next?" asked Hamlin.

Bob took some deep breaths trying to calm the panic rising up from his stomach.

Dale stepped forward. "I'll go."

Bob hadn't realized he had been holding his breath when Hamlin asked him, "Are you all right, boy? You look a bit pale."

Bob exhaled. "I'm fine. If you would lend me a needle and thread, I can make my own alterations."

"Captain Webb is very particular about how his soldier's uniforms fit. They are specially designed to enable you to be nimble and fast and move silently in the shadows. If your uniform isn't properly fitted, he will be in here yelling at me for doing a bad job. Now we can't have that, can we."

"I can assure you, I've been making my own clothes for years. I can come back and you can see for yourself if I've done the job properly."

"Are you sure you're up to it?" Hamlin's voice carried after Bob as he stepped away, his arms laden with the supplies: a bundle of uniform pieces, a paper packet of needles, and a spool of coarse black thread.

"Yes, sir," Bob said over his shoulder, forcing a calmness into his voice that belied the tightness in his chest. "I'll be back before lunchtime."

"See that you are. Otherwise, we'll both get into trouble."

Bob climbed the steps to the barracks. Pushing open the door, he was met with the cool, quiet dimness of the empty room. Rows of bunks stretched neatly on either side, each one identical and nothing out of place.

Sliding onto his bunk, Bob spread out the uniform on the straw mattress. He could see it was far different from the regular soldier's uniform. This was striking, a combination of practicality and pride that marked the Light Infantry as an elite force.

Bob worked quickly, his hands steady. The breeches were the easiest part. They were built for ease, meant to be pulled on and off without much trouble, and buttoned fast at the waist with a broad fall-front. He was pleased to see they were loose fitting in the crotch. He wouldn't have to worry about stuffing the breeches with a fake display of manhood.

Although Bob had worked hard to bind his chest, the risk of being discovered was ever-present. Every stitch had to be perfect, every fit exact, lest someone look too closely.

Bob pulled on the shirt quickly, then the waistcoat, thankful for its relaxed fit.

The coat fit reasonably well already, but he tucked the shoulders slightly, smoothing the fabric to create a more tailored appearance. His stitches were small and precise, honed by years of sewing his own clothes.

When the alterations were done, he stood before the small shard of polished tin propped against the wall near his bunk, examining his reflection. The uniform transformed him, erasing the small details that might have betrayed his true gender. He looked like any other soldier now, like Bob Shurtlieff, not Deborah Sampson.

Bob returned to the commissary to get Hamlin's approval of his alterations. Hamlin glanced up from his ledger as Bob entered.

"Let's see," he said gruffly, waving Bob forward.

Bob stood stiffly as Hamlin circled him, his hands tugging at the seams of the coat, checking the fit of his breeches.

"Well," he said finally, stepping back. "It's not bad. Not bad at all. You've got a steady hand; I'll give you that."

"Thank you, sir," Bob said, his voice careful, measured.

"Don't thank me," Hamlin muttered. "If Captain Webb's happy, I'll be happy."

Bob felt so proud in his new uniform. His relief was immediate, but fleeting.

As he walked towards the cookhouse, Bob froze in his tracks. William Bennett was walking directly towards him. He was unmistakable. Short, round, and in the same clothes he was wearing when he came to the Leonard's house with his marriage contract. Bob's pulse hammered in his ears as William moved through the milling soldiers, eyes sharp as a hawk scanning their faces.

Bob slipped behind a supply wagon, watching as William approached Richard and Dale standing near the barracks entrance.

"Have you seen a woman, about five foot ten, blond hair, blue eyes, and a long chin?" Her name is Deborah Sampson. She's my fiancée and might be dressed as a soldier. She'd dare such a thing, I swear it."

Richard eyed William skeptically. "A woman? Here at West Point impersonating a soldier? Mister, you must be daft or drunk."

"I'd pay good money to see that," said Dale, clearly amused.

"She might pass easily enough," William pressed, exasperated. She's tall, boyish enough in form. Have you seen anyone fitting that description?"

"She's not in our company," Richard said.

"We're Rangers, special forces," Dale added. "It wouldn't be possible for a woman to be disguised as a man and go unnoticed in such an elite company."

Bob pressed his back firmly against the wagon's rough wood, eyes closed briefly, chest tight. He could sense William's gaze sweeping the area again, reluctantly moving away. After an eternity, his footsteps faded.

That night, the barracks hummed with laughter and whispered speculations. Richard leaned back, grinning at the absurdity. "Imaging that, a woman dressed as one of us! She'd be braver than any soldier here to attempt something like that."

"Or mad," Dale chimed in, polishing his shoes. He cast a sly glance toward Bob. "Say Shurtlieff, come to think of it, you're tall enough, blond hair, blue eyes, and by God, that chin! You're not hiding something from us, are you?"

Bob laughed, loud and convincingly. "Aye, Dale, you've found me out," he joked boldly, spreading his arms wide. "Do I meet your lady's description? Should I fetch a dress and entertain you all?" His heart raced, but his voice didn't falter.

Laughter erupted around Bob, easing the tight coil in his stomach. Richard clapped him hard on the shoulder. "Sorry Shurtlieff, but you'd make the homeliest woman this side of the Hudson."

"Thanks for the compliment," Bob responded, forcing a grin, his nerves calming.

Bob lay back in his bunk as the others drifted into sleep, eyes fixed on the rafters, heart still beating swiftly. William Bennett's face lingered in his thoughts, unsettling and dangerous. He had been so close, far too close.

Bob began to pray silently.

As I wear this uniform, I ask for Your protection, wisdom, and guidance. Keep my resolve steady and my purpose clear. Help me to honor You with my actions and to serve with courage and integrity. I trust that You are with me on every step of this journey. In Your holy name, I pray. Amen.

Bob drew a deep breath, steeling himself. He would remain vigilant, ready. No man, not William Bennett, nor any other, would ever chain his spirit again.

As the camp fell into silence, Bob closed his eyes, his resolve stitched into the seams of his uniform, tight and unyielding.

CHAPTER 13

Armor Of God

MAY 29, 1782

The sharp trill of the fife jolted Bob awake, slicing through the pale haze of predawn light. He sat up quickly, his body stiff from the hard bunk and the ache of yesterday's efforts. Around him, the barracks stirred—men groaning and shuffling into motion, slipping into uniforms with the resigned efficiency of seasoned soldiers.

As he pulled on his uniform, scripture came to him unbidden. Ephesians 6:10—the Armor of God—each piece a sacred charge.

He fastened his belt. "May we stand and fasten the belt of truth about our waists."

Then the waistcoat. "May we put on the breastplate of righteousness."

Tying his shoes: "Make us ready to proclaim the gospel of peace."

His coat, heavy on his shoulders: "May we take up the shield of faith and use it to quench all the flaming arrows of the evil one."

Lastly, the cap. "May we take the helmet of salvation, and the sword of the Spirit, which is the Word of God."

He gave the coat a final tug and whispered with a half-grin, "Well, there it is. Armor on."

"Better move it, Shurtlieff!" Richard called from across the room, grinning as he adjusted his belt. "You don't want to be late on your first day as a Ranger."

"You go ahead," Bob replied, "I'll see you at the cookhouse." His voice steady despite the flutter in his chest. He strapped on his cartridge box and musket, checked the fit one last time, and stepped outside.

The necessary house backed up to the woods, but Washington had issued strict orders: no relieving oneself in the forest. Anyone caught disobeying risked thirty lashes. Bob had to risk it.

Dashing into the underbrush, he found a secluded thicket. His belt made quick work of his breeches. But anxiety twisted his stomach. Every snapping twig sent his heart hammering. He finished, wiped himself with a leaf, and crept back to the path.

He caught up with Dale and Richard. Together, they walked to the parade ground.

"You missed breakfast," Dale noted.

"Aren't you hungry?" Richard asked.

"Not really," Bob said. The knot in his stomach lingered.

The morning air was crisp and damp. The grass clung to their shoes, slick with dew, as the Light Infantry Company of the Fourth Massachusetts Regiment assembled. Captain Webb stood at the head. Beside him loomed Baron von Steuben, towering and immaculate in his blue and silver uniform, a silver-handled cane tapping against his palm as he surveyed them.

"You look ze part," Von Steuben declared in his thick German accent. "Now, ve vill see if you can act it."

The first drill began at the edge of camp, in a clearing. Grueling repetition filled the morning—marching, forming ranks, responding to commands with crisp precision.

"Left! Right! Forward! Von Steuben barked, his cane striking the earth like a metronome.

Bob focused on the rhythm, his shoes touching the ground in perfect unison with the men around him. Sweat prickled at his temples and his shoulders ached beneath the weight of his musket.

Richard stumbled, catching on a root. Von Steuben was there in an instant.

"Stand up straight!" he barked, his cane tapping against Richard's chest. "You vill not trip like a drunkard! Again!"

Richard flushed but recovered, steadying his step as the drill continued.

By midday, the men stood in rows, muskets at the ready. The sulfur stink of black powder hung in the air. The wooden targets, pocked with shot, bore silent testimony to their efforts.

"Load! Aim! Fire!" Von Steuben's commands rang over the crack of musket fire.

Bob moved smoothly—tear cartridge, pour powder, ram, prime, fire. Each motion sharpened by sweat and discipline. The musket bucked against his shoulder. He gritted through the jolt.

Dale reloaded with quiet fluidity. Richard, slower, showed growing confidence.

Von Steuben passed behind them. His cane tapped beside Bob.

"You shoot vell," he said. "But you must load faster. Again!"

Bob nodded, reloading with renewed urgency.

Later came the bayonet drill. Wooden dummies lined the clearing's edge. Von Steuben demonstrated, driving his bayonet into a target with ruthless efficiency.

"Zis is not for show," he declared. "Zis is for survival. You vill strike fast and true, or you vill die."

Bob lunged at his dummy, the bayonet striking home with a satisfying thunk.

"Good," Von Steuben said, passing by. "You vill do."

By sunset, the men returned to the barracks, dirt-streaked, sweat-drenched, exhausted.

Bob sat on his bunk, cleaning his musket. The repetitive motion soothed him.

"You looked good out there," Dale said, dropping onto the bunk beside him.

"Thanks," Bob replied, smiling faintly.

Richard leaned against the wall. "I thought Von Steuben was going to explode when I tripped. But I'll get it right tomorrow."

"We all will," Bob said, his resolve tightening.

As the barracks quieted, Bob offered a prayer of gratitude and slipped into sleep.

Days blurred into weeks. Drills became muscle memory. Captain Webb and Baron von Steuben sculpted them into something new—leaner, sharper, unyielding. Pain faded, pride remained.

One evening, under the glow of lantern light, Captain Webb stood before them. Silence fell.

"Men," Webb began. "You've learned discipline and trust. But tonight, everything changes."

Bob's muscles tensed. Richard and Dale stood still beside him.

"This isn't about firing volleys," Webb continued. "The Light Infantry exists for a different purpose. To move like ghosts. To gather intelligence. To decide who is friend or foe—without revealing yourselves."

Webb paused, letting the weight of his words sink in. "In Westchester County, the line between Loyalist and Patriot is a fine one, blurred by fear and opportunity. You will learn to tread it without faltering. You will master the art of stealth and reconnaissance. You will live on the lines, where the enemy is always closer than comfort allows." His voice dropped, his gaze steady. "If you fail, it is not just your life at stake but the lives of the men beside you."

The gravity of the moment settled heavily on them. Bob felt his stomach knot, a mixture of fear and determination twisting together. This was a challenge he could not afford to fail.

"Tonight, we begin in the classroom," Webb continued. "Then, under moonlight, you'll learn what it means to be Rangers."

The men gathered under canvas. Webb and Sgt. Munn spoke in low tones, teaching the art of silence—how to step without snapping twigs, how to read terrain, how to detect lies in a voice.

Bob memorized every word.

By nightfall, stars glimmered above the canopy. The forest whispered around them. Webb moved ahead, silent as smoke, demonstrating.

Bob mirrored him. Each step careful. Every breath controlled.

They practiced evasion, reconnaissance, camouflage. The forest became a test, its shadows full of lessons.

By dawn, they returned—mud-caked, breathless, but whole.

Webb gave a curt nod. "Rest."

Bob collapsed on his bunk. Every muscle screamed. But his secret was safe. His spirit, stronger.

Six weeks passed. Graduation loomed. They would cross the Hudson to Peekskill, into the wilds of Westchester.

But first came the storm.

It arrived past midnight—a distant rumble swelling into a sky-splitting roar. Rain pounded the barracks roof, wind howling like a beast in the dark.

Bob lay awake, eyes wide, heart racing. Then came the order.

"Up! Up, All of you! On your feet, packs on your backs!" Captain Webb's voice sliced the storm.

"Move it! Double-quick! You have two minutes!"

The barracks erupted. Bob strapped on his gear. Thirty pounds of steel, leather and wool slammed against his frame. Outside, the rain soaked them instantly.

"Form up!" Webb commanded. Lightning lit his face—grim and unreadable.

"This is your final test. Ten miles. Double-quick. Complete silence. If one fails, you all fail. Move out!"

They moved. Mud sucked at their feet. Thunder cracked above. Rain blinded them. The incline steepened, a near-vertical climb.

Bob clawed at the slope, fingers sinking into earth. Someone ahead slipped. Another hand caught him. No words. No thanks. Just the nod of survival.

Cold bit into bone. But they marched.

"We are Rangers!" Sgt. Munn roared. "Men of grit and iron will. We won't be beaten by a little rain!"

Finally, Webb raised his hand. They halted, back at camp.

Webb turned, rain streaking down his face. He studied them a moment. Then nodded.

"You are Rangers, one and all."

A cheer erupted.

"Tonight, you proved your mettle. Rangers do not quit. Remember that. Move faster. Fight harder. Survive longer. Not for me—but for yourselves."

Lightning flashed. They had done it. They were Rangers.

CHAPTER 14

Hunt For Delancey

JUNE 29, 1782

Dawn had scarcely broken when officers' voices cut through the camp, barking orders above the restless din of soldiers readying for the march to Westchester County.

Bob's company stood in formation, blue coats still damp from the storm. Packs slumped on aching shoulders. Bob adjusted his strap, glancing sideways at Richard and Dale. They looked just as sore and hollow-eyed as he felt after last night's punishing drills in the mud. But beneath the weariness, a quiet bond had taken root—forged by shared suffering and silent grit.

At the crack of a whip and the groan of wagon wheels, the regiment moved out, boots sucking into soft earth as they marched east toward King's Ferry. There, they'd cross the

Hudson and reenter the volatile wilderness of Westchester County.

By the time they reached the American lines at Peekskill, the regiment split. Bob's unit—the elite Light Infantry—received separate orders: march another ten miles south to the Croton River and establish camp on the fringe of the neutral zone, where no army held true control.

Two days later, Bob, Dale Lally, Richard Snow, and Roger Barrett were summoned to Captain Webb's tent.

"Colonel James Delancey has stolen a large haul of supplies, horses, cattle. He's moving them south to New York," Webb said. "Your orders are to locate his camp and confirm his presence."

Barrett's grin gave him away. Though untrained as a Ranger, he'd been placed in Webb's company for one reason—he was the only man in the company who could positively identify Delancey.

"Do you know where he's hiding, sir?" Barrett asked, barely containing his eagerness.

"Morrisania," Webb replied. "Enemy territory. The estate belonged to Lewis Morris, one of our own—signed the Declaration. The British seized it when they took New York City in '76. Morris has been serving in Congress in Philadelphia ever since."

Webb leaned in, his voice low. "Morrisania's well behind enemy lines. Just north of the City, across the Harlem River. They've turned it into a stronghold with redcoats, Tory irregulars, and patrols everywhere. None of our patrols has made it that far south. Until now, it's been considered too well guarded and too risky."

"However," Webb continued, "Washington believes this is a mission only the Rangers can handle. He needs confirmation that Delancey's there."

Richard exhaled. "Right into the lion's den, then, sir."

Webb nodded. "You four will accompany Ensign Towne on this mission. He's familiar with the terrain and has been to Morrisania once before the war. He'll brief you with further details. Prepare to leave at dawn. Dismissed."

Outside the tent, Towne pulled them aside. "You're going in as civilians. No uniforms. No muskets. Just knives, hidden out of sight. If we're caught, there must be no evidence we're soldiers."

They set out at first light, moving south through the Neutral Zone. They avoided the main roads but kept to the lesser lanes, passing burnt-out farms and hollowed villages where the war had left its mark and no one asked questions of strangers. Every mile carried them deeper into contested ground, and every step demanded caution.

By nightfall, they'd crossed into British-held territory. They left the lanes behind them, slipping into woods thick with shadows, following the bends of the Bronx River where the cover was deepest and no patrols would expect them.

As they neared the outskirts of the Morrisania estate, Towne raised a hand, signaling them to halt. The men crouched low, listening.

Through the break in the trees, torchlights flickered against the darkened walls of the manor house. Shadowy figures moved along the perimeter, sentries. Beyond them, the faint gleam of a stack of steel broadswords caught the firelight. Horses stood tethered near a cluster of outbuildings, their breath fogging in the chilly night air.

Towne handed Roger Barrett his spyglass. "See if you can identify Delancey or any of his men."

Barrett gripped the spyglass so tightly his knuckles were white with fury. "That's Delancey's men," he said, handing the glass back to Towne. "The two men near the barn shot my mother and sister."

"And Delancey?" Towne whispered.

Barrett shook his head. "Not outside."

"He's probably inside." Towne said, scanning the scene. The estate was a fortress in its own way: patrols shifting in a casual but constant rhythm, shoes crunching over the dirt paths between the barn and the main house, shadows moving behind the candlelit panes of the mansion's windows.

"We need to know their numbers for certain," Towne said under his breath. His gaze shifted to Lally and Barrett. "You two, get in closer. Find Delancey and see if you can find out what they're planning next. Dressed as civilians, like a lot of those men, no one should suspect you of not belonging."

Lally gave a quick nod towards Towne, adjusting his hat lower over his face. The two men slipped silently into the darkness, their forms barely discernible as they moved toward the outbuildings. The remaining three stayed crouched, scanning their surroundings for signs of anyone approaching them from any direction.

They all watched as Lally and Barrett had disappeared behind the far side of the house. For several agonizing minutes, all was silent but for the voices of Delancey's men sitting around the campfire.

Then, a sharp voice rang out. "Who goes there?"

Towne, Shurtlieff and Snow stiffened. A shadow moved near the barn. One of the sentries, stepping toward the outbuildings, musket in hand, went to investigate. The three Rangers were too far away to intervene. If Lally and Barrett were caught, there would be no saving them.

Then, movement. A flicker of motion from the barn's far side, barely perceptible in the dark. Barrett and Lally slipped out of the shadows, keeping to the far end of the field. They were heading back, fast. The sentry wasn't moving away. He was peering into the darkness, stepping forward to get a better look.

Lally did the only thing he could think of. With a quick flick of his wrist, he picked up a small rock and flung it hard to their left, hitting the wooden fence post with a sharp crack. The sentry hesitated, then stepped forward to investigate. But the rock's crack had done its work.

It was all the distraction Barrett and Lally needed. They silently bolted the last few yards into the brush where Bob and the other two men were waiting.

"Go!" Towne whispered.

They moved as one, slipping back into the darkness. There was no time for caution now, only speed and silence.

Once a safe distance away, Barrett was the first one to speak. "I saw him," he said softly.

"Delancey?" asked Towne.

Barrett nodded. "Upstairs window."

"That's what we needed to know. Let's hope he stays put." said Towne.

They reached camp the next morning and made their way toward Captain Webb's tent. Webb was already awake, standing over a crude wooden table beneath the tent's open flap, scanning a map of the neutral zone. He looked up as they approached, assessing their success before they had even spoken.

"I'm glad to see you all made it back in one piece," he said. "Did you find Delancey?"

"Yes, sir," Barrett said. "I saw him looking out the window."

"Excellent. What else did you discover?" Webb asked.

Towne stepped forward. "Lally and Barrett walked straight into their camp. No one suspected them. Lally managed to get close enough to overhear the men talking. We have confirmation of their numbers and their supply situation." He hesitated, then added, "and their next target."

Webb's brows lifted slightly. "Go on."

"They're planning a raid on our supply depot near Tarrytown," Lally said. "In two days."

"That gives us time. If we move quickly, we can turn this ambush against them." His gaze shifted to each of them. "You did well. Get some rest. You'll need it."

The company began their march the next morning at dawn towards Tarrytown. When they arrived, they set up their ambush along the narrow road leading to the supply depot, concealing themselves in the thick underbrush on either side of the path.

Bob's muscles ached from crouching for so long, his heart hammering in anticipation. Every sound, the rustling of leaves, the distant scream of an eagle, sent a prickle down his spine. He flexed his fingers around the stock of his musket, waiting. Then came the sound of hooves.

He tightened his grip as figures emerged. A column of riders moving cautiously. At the head of the party rode a man astride a beautiful bay colored horse, a stallion that gleamed, even in the dim light.

Webb lowered his spyglass with a gasp.

"True Briton!" Now for the first time he saw Colonel James Delancey. "So, you got your horse back."

Webb turned to the men and said, "That's Delancey in the front. His horse is called True Briton and is the property of the Army. I aim to get him back."

Just then, musket fire cracked from every direction. Shouts tore through the woods, horses reared and screamed, and the acrid stench of powder rolled thick in the air.

Bob lifted his musket and fired, the recoil jarring his shoulder. He dropped to one knee, reloading with the swift, practiced motions of instinct more than thought.

Through the smoke, Delancey charged. One of his riders leveled a pistol. The shot came—a thunderclap—and fire ripped through Bob's thigh. His leg gave way, dumping him into the dirt. White stars exploded in his vision. The world spun, but through the haze he saw the shooter grinning.

Rage surged. Bob's hands fumbled at his belt for his pistol, fingers slick with sweat, his mind screaming—move, fight.

A shadow blotted out the light. Delancey.

Without pause, he brought his saber down in a brutal arc aimed for Bob's neck.

Bob twisted at the last instant. Steel bit into his temple instead, carving fire across his skull. Hot blood poured into his eyes, blinding him.

Around him the chaos blurred—gunfire, hooves, men's voices. All of it narrowing to one pounding thought: They'll find out.

If he was taken to the surgeon, they'd strip off his uniform to tend to his wounds, then they would know. He had to end it now—before they discovered what lay beneath the uniform.

Bob's fingers curled around his pistol. It would be quick, a single shot. *Better this than dishonor.*

Before he could pull the trigger, strong hands clamped beneath his arms, dragging him backward. Blood blinded him, drenching his uniform.

"Sgt. Munn," Bob gasped.

"Hold on," Munn barked.

"No," Bob rasped. "Leave me. Save yourself."

"Not without you," Munn snapped.

Dale Lally appeared, panting, grabbing Bob's other arm. Together, they heaved Bob toward the saddle. But then–

A single shot rang out.

Bob felt it before he saw it, the way Lally's hands spasmed, then slackened, his grip slipping from Bob's body. Dale staggered back, his mouth open in silent shock.

He collapsed in the dirt, the life already gone from him. The ball had struck clean through his back and heart.

Bob twisted, just enough to glimpse smoke drifting from the trees, enemy shadows shifting in the haze.

Rage and grief surged in his chest, but his body gave way. Darkness closed in, swallowing him before he could even raise his pistol.

Solomon Beebe ran to help Sgt. Munn get Bob onto his horse and then knelt to see if anything could be done for Lally.

"Lally's gone Sgt.," said Beebe.

"Bring his body back to camp. I'm taking Shurtlieff to the surgeon's tent before he bleeds to death."

When Bob came to, he was no longer on the battlefield. He lay on a hard cot beneath the glow of a dim lantern. Low murmurs of wounded men filled the French surgeon's tent. A large bandage covered his forehead where the doctor had stitched up his head wound.

Bob turned his focus to the agony in his thigh. The bullet was still there lodged deep in muscle. He could feel it—an ugly, foreign thing that did not belong in him.

To keep his identity secret, he'd have to dig it out himself. Rising dizzily from the cot, he searched through the supplies on the surgeon's table for something to remove the bullet. Getting what he needed, he headed back to his cot. His fingers, slick with sweat, curled around the stolen needle and thread. A curved silver probe gleamed in the lamplight.

"Please, God, give me strength."

Bob clenched a scrap of leather between his teeth. He forced the probe into the wound, biting down as agony flared through his leg like fire. The metal scraped against the bullet, sending jolts of pain up his spine, his vision blurring at the edges.

He didn't scream. His body trembling as he twisted the probe. A final wrenching pull and the bullet slid free. His hands were shaking as he threaded the needle with blood-slick fingers. Stitching the wound closed, clumsily but determined, every stab of the needle sending white-hot agony through him.

By the time he finished, he could barely sit upright, his uniform soaked in blood.

The curtain at the entrance parted. The French doctor stepped inside, eyes narrowing as they fell on the bloodied fabric clinging to Bob's leg. "You have another wound," he said flatly. "It needs stitching."

"It's just a scratch," Bob rasped. "Nail in the saddle."

The doctor stared at him for a long, considering moment. Then, with a shake of his head, he turned and walked out.

Bob let himself slump back against the cot, eyes sliding shut against the pain. He had survived. His secret was safe, for now. Then, he remembered Dale being shot in the back. He swallowed hard, his throat thick with grief. He lay on his cot, pressing his trembling hands together, fingers bloodied and raw as he prayed.

"Lord, please welcome Dale home as the warrior he was. May he now rest in peace, the kind we never find in this world but only with You in Heaven. Amen."

He lay down his head, staring at the flickering lantern above him. The pain of the loss of his friend pressing against his ribs, sharper than any wound.

For the first time since Dale had fallen, Bob let the tears come.

CHAPTER 15

Snow Falls

OCTOBER 9, 1782

The Rangers moved through the forest like wraiths; their passage marked only by the whisper of branches brushing against wool and leather. Ensign Towne, ever watchful, lifted his hand. The company froze. Ahead, two figures stood by a rough barricade of crates and barrels, their lanterns pushing back the dark in a weak, trembling glow.

One man, tall and angular, cradled a musket with easy familiarity, his expression unreadable in the dim light. Beside him, a wiry sentry shifted restlessly, fingers drumming a nervous rhythm against his thigh. Both carried themselves with the alertness of men accustomed to danger.

Towne stepped forward, his tone casual, measured. "Evening, lads."

The taller man raised his musket, eyes narrowing. "Who goes there?"

Towne let a thin smile curve his lips. "Name's Towne. Delancey sent us to collect supplies—he's planning a move come morning."

The men exchanged a quick glance. Suspicion lingered, but the detail was just plausible enough.

"Where are the supplies?" Towne asked.

"In the back of the cave," the tall one said, pulling aside a tarp to reveal the entrance.

Towne peered inside and gave a soft whistle. "Well, you've saved us a job. I'd never have found that in the dark."

"That's all of it," the sentry replied.

That was all the confirmation the Rangers needed.

Shadows slipped from the trees, rifles leveled. The sentries stiffened, eyes going wide as realization struck—these were no allies. One dropped the tarp and bolted for the woods, dragging his companion with him.

A few Rangers moved as if to give chase, but Towne held them back with a curt gesture. "Let them run. They'll tell Delancey soon enough, and that's exactly what we want. He'll come looking—and we'll be ready. Now, no time to waste. Load up what you can, especially the powder."

The Rangers tore into the stockpile, shoving what they could onto carts and into their packs. The march back was swift and silent. But something was wrong. Snow stumbled.

Bob caught him before he could collapse completely, his forehead damp with fever. "You're burning up."

"Just need…" Snow coughed violently, sagging against Bob. "A minute."

Ensign Towne hesitated. "We can't stop."

Bob squared his shoulders. "I'll stay with Snow. Get him rested, then bring him back."

Towne nodded in agreement and the company moved on.

Bob dragged Snow toward the nearest farmhouse.

Abraham Van Tassel greeted them at the door. "You Patriots?"

Bob nodded. "My friend is sick. We need shelter."

Van Tassel stepped aside. "Come in."

The bolt slid into place the moment they crossed the threshold. Bob felt something was wrong but they had no choice.

"We don't have any beds left, but we do have a garret you could sleep in," said Van Tassel.

"Anything will do. My friend needs to rest," said Bob.

Van Tassel's fifteen-year-old daughter, Mary, came into the room holding a candle. "What's going on, Father? Who are these men?"

"They're soldiers who need a place to spend the night," he said. "Show them to the garret."

"But father, there's nothing in there. Wouldn't they be better off in the barn?" she asked.

"Do as I say, Mary."

"Yes, Father."

Mary led the way. Snow could barely walk. Bob dragged him up the stairs, his muscles aching with each heave of his comrade's weight. The room was little more than a forgotten space beneath the eaves. The cracks in the walls were stuffed with old flour sacks in a feeble attempt to keep out the creeping fingers of winter.

Rats scurried at their intrusion, their tiny claws clicking against the bare floorboards before disappearing into the dark corners. The sound of their restless movements sent a shudder through Bob's spine. Snow let out a wheezing groan, his body sagging against him. With a grunt of effort, Bob eased him down onto the cold floor, the wood unforgiving beneath Snow's fever-ravaged frame.

Mary handed the candle to Bob as she turned to leave. "I'm sorry about this."

"It'll do. Thank you."

Snow began coughing violently as Mary closed the door. His breath rattled in his chest; his skin was clammy. Bob pressed a hand to his forehead, *too hot and too far gone*, he thought.

Snow's eyes were filled with fear. "Bob, I want to apologize to you for mocking your faith in God. I never understood how people could put so much stock in something they can never touch or see, until now."

"Snowman, true Faith is when you believe with all your heart without seeing," said Bob.

"I don't think I've got much time," said Snow coughing and gasping for air at the same time. "Will you pray for me?"

Bob took Snow's hand, rough and burning in his grip, and closed his eyes. "Lord above," he said softly, "this man comes before You in pain and fear. But You know his heart. You've seen his courage, his struggle, his kindness, even when cloaked in pride. Forgive him. Welcome him. Replace his fear with peace, his sorrow with hope. Let him walk into Your light and rest in Your love. Amen."

Bob felt the weight of Snow's hand slacken in his palm, and in that moment, the pain, the war, the suffering—all faded. There was only the man who once cracked jokes during drills, the friend who'd finally found peace.

Snow's lips parted as if to reply—but only a final breath escaped. A small sigh. And then... stillness.

A low murmur of voices rose from the floor below. Bob pressed his eye to a thin crack between the garret boards and froze.

"Our supplies have been stolen," said Delancey, his tone sharp with fury. "But I know who did it and I'll make them pay."

"I may have two of the thieves in my garret. One is very ill and the other one is walking with a limp. They were left here so the sick man could get some rest. He looks like he'll be resting permanently soon," said Van Tassel grinning.

"I want to question them," said Delancey. "We're going to attack their camp at dawn."

Bob pulled back, heart thudding. Snow was dead. And now he would be too—unless...

A light knock stirred him. Mary appeared in the doorway with a tin cup of water. "I'm sorry. There's no bread but here's some water."

Bob met her gaze. "Help me. Please. Those men below are going to kill me."

"What about your friend?" she asked.

"He's gone. I'll come back for him. Is there another way out?"

"You can climb out the window in my room."

Bob followed her through the house like a ghost. At the windowsill he paused, whispering, "Thank you."

Bob leapt silently into the night and crept around the side of the house. There, tied to the post, was True Briton, Delancey's prize horse. The great stallion met his gaze with a knowing look.

Bob swung himself into the saddle. Grief and rage surged like wildfire in his chest. He rode through the night, the wind tearing through his coat. When he reached camp, he burst into Munn's tent.

"Snow's dead," he gasped, shaking Sgt. Munn awake. "And Delancey's coming at dawn."

Munn sat bolt upright. "Then we better get to him first."

The entire company rode back with Bob, waiting until the house was still. Delancey's men drank themselves into a stupor. At midnight, the Rangers struck.

The fight was quick. Most of Delancey's men were asleep in the barn. The Rangers were on them before they even reached for their weapons. They were all captured without a single casualty. Van Tassel was dragged from his house. Mary watched from the front door of the house as her father was taken away. "Please don't hurt him," she pleaded.

"I'll see he's treated fairly," said Bob.

Bob stormed through the house, his heart hammering. A window at the back was open, the chilly night wind fluttering the curtains. The hoofprints were fresh, still steaming, like the devil himself had vanished into the woods. Delancey had escaped by mere minutes.

Bob cursed under his breath. Delancey was like a snake, slithering through their fingers repeatedly. But next time, there would be no escape.

By dawn, the prisoners were bound, Van Tassel marched alongside them. Bob put Snow's body on the back of True Briton and carried him back to camp.

That night, beneath the pale moon, the Rangers claimed a small, necessary victory. But the war with Delancey was far from over.

CHAPTER 16

The Widow Hunt

DECEMBER 13, 1782

The road that ran alongside the Croton River was treacherous, winding through the neutral zone where neither side held firm control. Bob and three other Rangers from the Light Infantry were moving cautiously, their muskets at the ready. Suddenly, the silence was shattered by the thunder of hooves. A small scouting party from the Dutch Cavalry burst from the tree line, swords gleaming in the pale light.

"Ambush!" Bob shouted, diving for cover as musket fire erupted around them. The four men returned fire, felling two of their attackers, but the rest pressed forward. Outnumbered and outflanked, they had no choice but to retreat. Racing toward the Croton ferry, they reached the dock and found a Dutch ferry pilot about to leave to go home.

"We need passage now!" Bob demanded, grabbing the man by his coat. When the pilot objected, Bob pressed his pistol to the man's temple. "Now!"

Fearful for his life, the ferry pilot relented, guiding them onto the small craft. The river's current was strong, and the night air bit through their clothes as they drifted toward the sandbar. Before they could reach the far bank, the pilot refused to go any further.

"This is as far as I can take you," he said, eyes wide with terror.

With no other choice, the four men struggled through the chest-deep, icy water until they reached the shore. Shivering and exhausted, they made their way to the Widow Hunt's tavern, their only hope for shelter.

The widow welcomed them with a smirk, her silver hair neatly pinned under a bonnet. "Brave soldiers," she crooned, "you must be half-frozen. Sit by the fire. We're nearly out of food for the night. I'll send my servant George for refreshments."

Something in her voice didn't ring true. Bob had learned to read people well, and her hospitality seemed forced, her gaze shifting too quickly. As George shuffled away, Bob stood abruptly.

"She's lying," he whispered to his men. "We've got to get out of here now!"

"What do you mean?" Private Wheeler asked.

"Trust me. There's no time to waste."

The men exchanged wary glances before rising as one. Bob led the way out, slipping into the night just as George disappeared down the road. Moments later, they intercepted the old man.

"Hello, George. My name is Bob Shurtlieff. Tell me, where are you really going?"

George hesitated but then sighed. "Widow Hunt said I was to fetch Colonel Delancey so he can capture you fellas. He's camped down at the end of this lane."

"You may have just saved our lives. I can't offer much, but if you want to come with us—you'd be a free man"

"That's mighty kind of you, sir," George replied. "But that's not exactly what you're offering me is it? The freedom you're fighting for is freedom for white folks so they don't have to pay taxes to the king. It's not freedom from slavery for Black folks. Even if Widow Hunt gave me papers saying I was free, any white man could come along, tear up that piece of paper and take me to the South to pick cotton, where I'd be beaten and starved. I'd be worse off than ever before."

"I understand. You're a good and wise man, George. I'm so pleased to have met you," said Bob.

"Pleasure to have met you too. I hope you get back safely," said George.

"Thanks again for warning us about Delancey," said Bob.

"You're welcome." George continued walking slowly down the lane to Delancey's camp.

The wind howled through the leafless trees as Bob and his three companions pressed forward along the muddy path leading away from the Widow Hunt's tavern. They needed to disappear before Delancey and his men could catch their scent.

"We need to put as much distance between us and that tavern as quick as possible," Bob muttered, quickening his pace. "Delancey won't be far behind."

The men nodded in silent agreement. Their uniforms were damp from the river crossing, and the chill bit at their bones, but they pushed on. Bob glanced over his shoulder. He could see George moving slowly towards Delancey's camp. He hoped his kindness towards the old man had at least left some mark on the servant's heart and that he would send Delancey in the wrong direction.

When George got back, Widow Hunt was angry. "They've gone. Did you see them? Did they say where they're going?"

"No, ma'am," George replied. "I didn't see anybody. They must have gone in a different direction."

Delancey showed up with his men. "Where are the soldiers?" demanded Delancey.

"They just up and left. I was in the kitchen and never heard them leave," said Widow Hunt.

"They can't be far off," said Delancey. "There's only two ways they can go. Half of you come with me. We'll head down to the river. The rest of you search every house and outbuilding from here leading into the forest."

In the shadows beyond the farm, Bob and the Rangers pressed deeper into the night, moving fast and silent.

"Where do we head now?" asked Private Andrews.

"There's an old mill a few miles upriver," Private Wheeler answered. "It belonged to a Patriot who fled when the British took the area. If it's still standing, it should give us cover for the night."

"We can't risk it. We've got to cross the river now," said Bob. "Delancey and his men won't come across the river after us tonight. But, if we stay on this side, he'll surely track us down."

Being able to disappear without leaving a trail is what the Rangers were trained to do. Every snap of a twig, every rustling leaf served to heighten their awareness. The distant sound of hooves on frozen ground sent a jolt of fear through them.

"They're coming," whispered Private Hayes.

The four men scattered, pressing themselves into the undergrowth as Delancey and the rest of his men passed along the road, heading towards the river. The riders carried torches, their flickering flames illuminating the darkness in brief, golden flashes. Bob held his breath as Delancey himself rode by; his face set in a determined scowl.

"They couldn't have gotten far," Delancey growled to his men. "Fan out! I want them found before sunrise."

The riders split into groups, heading in different directions along the beach. The four Rangers remained frozen in place as hooves trampled the ground nearby. Finally, when the sounds began to fade into the distance, Bob gave a quiet signal.

The Rangers knew that their only path back to the American lines was the same treacherous river they had crossed earlier. The ferryman had used a rope to pilot the ferry back and forth across the river. The crescent moon gave off just enough light to enable them to find the rope and pull themselves across to the other side. It was a dangerous feat that even the strongest of men would have struggled with. The frayed rope stretched from one bank to the other, a lifeline against the rushing current. One by one, the men grasped the rope and began pulling themselves across. Bob was the last to go.

Midway through, the current surged, tearing his grip from the rope. The freezing water swallowed him, dragging him under. Panic clawed at his chest, but then he closed his eyes and prayed. "God save me!"

A bright light illuminated the water around him. Bob suddenly felt completely calm and at peace. He stopped struggling. Miraculously, his fingers found the rope. Kicking hard, he pulled himself up, gasping for air. With one final effort, he reached the bank, where his comrades dragged him onto solid ground. Cold, weary, but alive, Bob said simply, "Thank you, Lord for delivering me from a watery grave."

They made their way back to camp, found Sgt. Munn, and reported everything they had learned. The Widow Hunt's deception, and the location of Delancey's encampment would prove invaluable in the ongoing effort to capture Delancey.

Lying on his cot, Bob drew in a breath, the weight of the night's trials settling heavy on his chest. He reflected on his meeting with George, who had put a whole new perspective on this war for freedom. *Now I understand why Phyllis Wheatley had gotten so angry with me. She's right. I was only looking at this fight for freedom from a white man's point of view. Dear Lord, may it be Your will that one day all people, no matter their color, will be free to live as they choose.*

Bob had faced death twice that day, and by Divine Providence, he had been spared. It was no coincidence. Bob felt it in the marrow of his bones. He believed God's hand was upon him, upon them all, and was reassured that the war they were fighting was righteous. But there was no time for revelry. Delancey was still loose, and the battle for independence was far from over.

CHAPTER 17

Reign Of Terror Ends

DECEMBER 27, 1782

Captain Webb sent a report of the recent incident with his men and their encounter with Delancey and Widow Hunt up the chain of command, where it landed on the desk of General Washington.

"Delancey must be stopped," said General Washington to his aide-de-camp, Lieutenant Colonel Tench Tilghman. "Send word to Captain Webb that his primary duty now is to find Delancey and rid Westchester County of him and his raiders."

"Yes, General," Tilghman replied.

The order from General Washington arrived with the weight of Divine Justice. Captain Webb read it aloud to his gathered men. A righteous fire ignited in the eyes of his Rangers. They had seen the havoc Delancey's men had wrought: burned farms, stolen cattle, lives destroyed. Now was the time for retribution.

The next day, Captain Webb ordered Sgt. Munn to bring Bob to see him.

"Shurtlieff, we are going after Delancey. Reports place him back at Morrisania. We'll draw him out, and you—on True Briton—will be the bait. Half the company will ride with you, the other half with me. We'll surround the house and block every escape route. This ends now."

Bob swallowed, masking his unease. "I'm ready, sir."

"Sgt. Munn, have the men ready to move out in an hour."

"Yes, Captain."

"Dismissed."

Back at his tent, Bob pulled his Bible from his haversack and read from Psalm 18:

I will pursue my enemies and overtake them; I will not turn back until they are destroyed. I will crush them, and they will fall beneath my feet. For You girded me with strength for war, and made my adversaries bow before me. You deliver me from my enemies; You exalt me above those who rise against me. You rescue me from the unrighteous man. Thank You, Lord.

The memory of Dale Lally being shot in the back by Delancey's man burned in Bob's mind as he tightened True Briton's saddle. The sting of Van Tassel's betrayal—Snow's death, Widow Hunt's false Patriot mask—sharpened his resolve.

With Bob in the lead, the Rangers rode out under cover of fog. The woods south of the Croton River closed around them like a cathedral, the mist ghosting over the hills. At Morrisania, Loyalist marauders lounged around the estate, unaware that Webb's Rangers—America's most feared fighters—were encircling them.

Through his spyglass, Bob saw Webb signal from the flank. Bob raised his hand in return. Then, like wraiths rising from the fog, the Rangers descended.

Muskets cracked, sharp and sudden. Bob drove True Briton straight through the chaos, his bayonet flashing as he clashed with a Loyalist sentry. The man swung wildly—Bob ducked and drove his blade home. A scream cut short.

Panic swept the camp. Horses reared, breaking their tethers; tents collapsed as men scrambled for weapons. Delancey burst from the house, barking orders. His eyes widened when he saw True Briton.

"That's my horse!" Delancey roared. "I want him back!"

"Come and get him," Bob shot back, grinning defiantly.

Delancey fired his pistol—but at that moment Sgt. Munn slammed the weapon aside with his musket butt. The shot went wide.

"Arrgh!" shouted Delancey as he turned his horse to try to outrun the Rangers.

"Delancey's getting away!" Bob shouted.

True Briton lunged forward like lightning, his hooves barely touching earth. Bob bent low over the stallion's neck, giving chase.

Delancey lashed his horse, his eyes wild. He knew as well as anyone—if he was caught, there would be no mercy.

At the ridge ahead, musket fire cracked. Webb and his men blocked the escape. Delancey's horse reared. Surrounded on all sides, Delancey's reign of terror ended in a circle of drawn muskets.

Delancey bared his teeth like a cornered wolf, his men behind him wavering between fight and flight. Webb rode forward, unflinching.

"Colonel Delancey," Webb said, his voice carrying in the sudden stillness. "You don't deserve mercy. You and your men have murdered innocent people and driven families from their homes. You have one choice—leave Westchester County now and never return. Refuse, and we will shoot you where you stand. What will it be?"

Delancey's jaw tightened. His gaze flicked to Bob astride True Briton, to the grim faces of the Rangers, their muskets steady. Finally, Delancey gave a curt nod. "We will go."

"Wise choice," Webb said. "We'll escort you to your home at West Farms to collect your family. From there, we'll see you and your men to New York City limits. If any man tries to escape, we'll shoot you all. And know this—your property will be destroyed so you'll have no reason to return."

Delancey turned to his men. "None of my men will try to escape."

The procession moved south. Delancey and his raiders rode silent, flanked by Rangers with muskets raised. Westchester County was free again; the land bathed in the last glimmer of sunlight. Bob looked skyward. "Dear Lord," he murmured, voice rough, "thank You for this victory. All glory and honor is Yours, now and forever. Amen."

Several Rangers echoed softly, "Amen."

The Rangers pressed forward, escorting Delancey and his broken men, away from the land they had tormented. Bob knew this was more than just a victory, it was justice, long overdue. The Revolutionary War for Independence was nearly over.

When they reached West Farms, Delancey helped his young pregnant wife, Martha, into a carriage driven by his slave, Tom, and sent her ahead toward the city. Surrounded on all sides by Webb's Rangers, Delancey, and the rest of his men, followed. Bob lingered at the rear, watching as Delancey crossed the city's border—his reign ended, his shadow at last lifted from the land.

CHAPTER 18

The General's Orderly

DECEMBER 28, 1782

The dim glow of a lantern flickered against the canvas walls of the tent, casting long shadows, as Captain Webb sat hunched over his desk, quill scratching furiously across parchment. Bob stood at attention, his posture rigid, despite the exhaustion creeping into his bones.

Webb glanced up, his sharp eyes locking onto Bob.

"You courageously led the charge against Delancey and his men. That kind of courage doesn't go unnoticed."

"Just doing my duty, sir," said Bob humbly.

Webb let out a chuckle, shaking his head as he penned the final words on the report.

"Duty or not, General Paterson will want to hear of our victory today as soon as possible."

Webb folded the document, sealing it with a firm press of wax.

"You're to take this report to General Paterson. He's in Newburgh with General Washington. Pack all your gear and take True Briton with you. He's the fastest horse in the county. Also, Lt. Col. Tilghman wants the horse back. Two of Delancey's men stole True Briton from him in Philadelphia. You are to leave immediately."

"Yes, sir," Bob said, with a look of concern on his face.

"We will be breaking camp in the morning and moving back across the river to the cantonment at New Windsor. Once you've delivered this dispatch, you will report to Ensign Towne, who is already at New Windsor."

Captain Webb noticed Bob's hesitation. "What is it, Shurtlieff? Feeling tired are you?"

"No, sir. I'm fine, but True Briton may not be. He's been running hard all day and I'm not sure he's up to the trip without a bit of rest."

"You know, I was warned about you by Captain Thorpe. He said you were insubordinate and questioned his judgement regarding one of his recruits. He almost didn't accept you into the army."

"Sir, a young boy was deathly ill and I offered to take him to the surgeon's tent. I was told if I did so, that I was not to come back. I stepped back to my place in line. After we were dismissed. I found the boy in the forest and he died in my arms."

"Enough. Captain Thorpe was right. You are insubordinate. You will take True Briton and get this dispatch to headquarters as fast as possible. Understood?"

"Yes, Captain."

Before mounting, Bob spoke to True Briton. "I know you're tired boy, but we've got to get this dispatch to headquarters. It's about you, boy and what a terrific job you did today helping us capture Delancey. Now, you've got to shine one more time and run like the wind to Newburgh. Then I promise you can have a well-deserved rest."

Captain Webb and Sgt. Munn stood silent as Bob and True Briton vanished into the night at a gallop. The hour was ten when they left the camp near the Croton, riding north beneath a bright, full moon.

The Albany Post Road stretched ahead of them. Their path would take them to Fishkill, where the ferry waited to carry them over the Hudson to Newburgh. Nearly thirty miles lay ahead, hard ground, but clear enough beneath the moon's gaze. An ordinary horse would take four hours to make it, if he made it at all. But there was no horse like True Briton, He could do it in three. They would not stop until the Hudson River lay behind them.

The moon shone bright as Bob let True Briton stretch out into a gallop, eating up the miles beneath him. The rush of speed was exhilarating for them both. Sweat lathered the great horse's flanks, but his stride stayed strong, steady, relentless.

They had covered nearly fifteen miles when disaster struck. A sharp clatter, then a sudden falter in True Briton's stride. The horse stumbled, nearly pitching Bob from the saddle before pulling up lame, favoring one leg.

Bob reined him in hard and swung down. "Whoa, boy. Easy now. Easy."

He crouched beside the great horse, running a steady hand down the trembling leg. The shoe was gone, torn clean off. The edge of the hoof was cracked and bleeding. There was no fixing it here. No farrier, no forge, no help.

"I know it hurts, boy" sighed Bob. "But we have to keep going."

They weren't going any farther at speed. In order to reach Newburgh, they'd have to do it walking slowly together. Bob gathered the reins and turned toward the road. True Briton whickered softly and nosed at his shoulder. Bob gave him a tired smile and started forward, one foot in front of the other.

By the time they reached Newburgh, the sun was already climbing high in the sky. Bob's legs ached from the long walk; True Briton limped beside him, head hanging low.

At the edge of the camp, a shout rang out. "Halt! Who goes there?"

The sentries stepped forward, muskets raised. They didn't lower them until Bob gave his name and stated his orders.

"Private Shurtlieff. I'm a Ranger with the Light Infantry Company of the Fourth Massachusetts Regiment. I have an urgent dispatch from Captain Webb for General Paterson."

One of the men gave him a weary look. "The General's quarters are near the back on the left side of the camp."

"Thank you." Turning towards True Briton, Bob said, "Let's go boy. We're nearly there."

Bob approached a sentry standing guard outside a tent.

"I have an urgent dispatch for General Paterson. Can you direct me to his quarters?"

"This is General Paterson's tent. He's not here at the moment," replied the sentry.

"It's news of a victory," Bob said.

Just then, the flap of the general's tent opened and a soldier came out. "I'm General Paterson's orderly; I'll take the dispatch."

Bob looked in astonishment at the soldier. "Beebe, is that you?"

"Shurtlieff? So, you survived Tarrytown after all," said Beebe.

"Thanks to you for getting me onto Sgt. Munn's horse and Sgt. Munn getting me to the surgeon," replied Bob.

"Too bad about Lally. He didn't make it," replied Beebe.

"I was devastated when they told me. He was like a brother to me," said Bob.

"He was a great soldier and a brave man," said Beebe.

"Yes, he was. I miss him terribly," Bob said. "After Tarrytown, you seemed to just disappear. I wondered what happened to you. So, tell me, how did you come to be working for General Paterson?"

"When we got back to camp, Captain Webb told me to take a dispatch about what happened at Tarrytown to General Paterson. He also said to take all my gear with me as I was being re-assigned to a new duty station. Apparently, one of the general's orderlies was ill and the general asked for me to be assigned to him. I'm from Berkshire County and Paterson's wife was friends with my Aunt Mavis. She'd written to Mrs. Paterson asking to get me assigned to the General's staff. You can imagine my surprise when I got here and was asked if I'd like to serve on the general's staff as an orderly!"

"You mean to say you had a choice?" asked Bob.

"Incredible, isn't it! General Paterson only wants people around him that are truly dedicated to the job and to him," said Beebe. "Needless to say, I was thrilled to be asked and immediately accepted the position."

"Man, what I wouldn't give for a job like that!"

"Anything's possible. I know you're a man of faith, so pray about it," said Beebe.

"I certainly will. Say, can you tell me where I can find a farrier. This is Delancey's prize horse, True Briton. He threw a shoe on our way here and he's in a bad way."

"There's a stable at the end of the lane. The blacksmith is there."

"Thanks so much. It's great to see you again Beebe."

"I'm glad to see you're still among the living. I hope your horse will be OK."

"I fear his racing days are over for good."

"He's a beautiful bay and looks like he's still got a lot of life left in him."

"Let's hope so. Beautiful Bay. That would be a great name for him," said Bob. "Thanks, Beebe. I'll stay in the barn with the horse until he gets seen to," replied Bob. "Then I'm supposed to report to Ensign Towne at the New Windsor cantonment."

"Alright. See you around," said Beebe.

Bob led True Briton down the path to the stable. The steady clang of metal on metal rang out as the blacksmith worked in the yard.

The smith looked up as they approached, wiping his hands on his apron. His gaze went straight to the horse's injured hoof.

Thrown a shoe, has he? Looks like he's traveled a fair way on it."

"From Croton," Bob said. "He needs looking after."

The blacksmith nodded. "That's a long way for a lame horse." He stepped forward, running his hand down the leg with practiced care. "You're lucky it's not worse."

Bob gave a tired nod. "Can you put him right?"

I can. Won't take me long. Let him cool off while I heat the iron." The blacksmith pointed toward the water trough. "Give him a drink. I'll have him sorted soon enough."

Bob stroked True Briton's neck. "You hear that, boy? Help's come at last."

The blacksmith smiled. "He's a strong one. Got spirit, too, by the look of him."

"How long before he's fit to ride again?" Bob asked.

"You can ride him, slow and steady tomorrow," the smith said. "No hard galloping for a day or two. Let the hoof settle. After that, he'll be sound as ever."

Bob nodded. "Slow and steady it is."

A young corporal came into the corral. "Are you Bob Shurtlieff?" he asked.

"Yes, I am."

"You're wanted by General Paterson."

"Be right there," he said, before turning to the blacksmith. "Thank you for taking care of him."

"That's what I do," the smith grinned.

Bob headed toward the command tent. The General, a tall imposing man with steel-gray hair, was reading the dispatch when Bob entered. He looked up, sharp eyes assessing.

"Shurtlieff?"

"Yes, sir."

"Captain Webb speaks highly of you and the role you played in capturing Delancey using his prize racehorse as bait."

Bob's chest tightened. "Thank you, sir. I was just one of many men who fought hard to take down Delancey, a truly evil man."

"I have deep respect for a man who shows such courage in battle. I'm in need of an orderly. Would you like to work for me?" asked the general. "You'd be assigned here as part of my staff. However, it's a voluntary position, you can choose not to accept it if you'd rather stay with your company."

Bob was almost speechless. He took a deep breath, exhaled slowly, and replied, "I'd be honored, sir."

One more thing, Paterson drew out a short braid of green and white cord, rough but carefully woven, from a small chest on his desk.

"Among the Rangers, we keep our own tokens. This cord is given when a soldier stands his ground, no matter the odds.

It is not for show, but for you to wear beneath your sleeve, a private reminder of what you've accomplished."

He looped the braid once around Bob's wrist and tied it snugly, the threads pressing against the skin before he tugged the cuff down to hide it.

"Your name will be carried in the rolls of this regiment. Among your brothers, your service will be remembered."

Bob bowed his head. "I am honored, sir. Thank you, for this token, and for a place among your men."

"I also understand you've brought Delancey's prize horse with you," said Paterson. "Lt. Col. Tench Tilghman is excited to get him back."

"I'm afraid he threw a shoe on the way here but the farrier is seeing to it at the moment," replied Bob.

"Luckily, he didn't break his leg. It would have been a shame to have to put down such a remarkable horse," said the general.

"Indeed, it would, sir."

"See Sgt. Beebe. He'll get you set up with everything you'll need. Welcome to my command. You're dismissed."

"Thank you so much, sir. I won't disappoint you."

Beebe was waiting when Bob stepped out of the general's tent. He took one look at Bob's face and gave a knowing nod.

"Well, I take it congratulations are in order."

"Looks that way," Bob smiled.

Beebe offered his hand and Bob shook it without hesitation.

"You've earned it," Beebe said. "None better."

"Thank you."

Beebe released his grip and said, "Come on, then. I'll show you where everything stands, who's who, what's where. Get you familiar with the place."

"I'm grateful for your help in getting me settled in," Bob said.

As they walked, Bob felt the weight of his new job settle on his shoulders, not the burden, but the responsibility. This wasn't the kind of post handed out lightly. It had been earned, and he would be sure to keep it.

In the days that followed, Bob settled into his new duties with quiet determination. Among his responsibilities, he was frequently tasked with couriering messages and reports between various commands, including direct deliveries to General Washington.

On one such occasion, Bob arrived at Washington's headquarters to deliver an important report. As he handed the document to Lt. Col. Tench Tilghman, the officer's hand brushed against Bob's and he felt the cord tied around Bob's wrist.

"Is that cord under your sleeve from General Paterson?"

"Yes, sir. General Paterson gave it to me for helping to capture James Delancey."

"What's your name soldier?" Tilghman asked.

"Bob Shurtlieff, sir."

"I read about you in the dispatch from Captain Webb. I understand you actually stole True Briton out from under his nose and used him as bait to get Delancey out in the open."

"Yes, sir. He was none too happy to see me riding his horse."

"Oh, I can imagine. I once raced against him at Newmarket in New Jersey. Needless to say, True Briton flew down the track leaving the rest of us choking on his dust. I've never seen a horse run like him. It looked as if his hoofs barely touched the ground as he ran. After the race, I spoke to Delancey about bringing True Briton to Maryland to bring new life into our stock. Delancey laughed and said he was strictly for his stock alone and no one would ever ride True Briton but him."

"On my way here to bring the dispatch to General Paterson from Captain Webb, I was told to ride him flat out in order to get here as quickly as possible. It was as if we were flying with the wind and was the most exhilarating ride of my life. It all came to a halt when he threw a shoe."

"I heard about that."

"I think his racing days may be over."

"I suggest you ride him for now and keep an eye on him for me."

"Thank you, sir. I'll take really good care of him."

True Briton healed quickly. Bob rode him daily delivering messages and dispatches between Washington's headquarters at Newburgh, to the cantonment at New Windsor and down to West Point, fifteen miles away.

General Paterson's kindness had made Bob feel seen, valued, almost safe. But safety was an illusion. With the army dissolving around him, Bob's carefully built world was about to shatter.

CHAPTER 19

Trouble With The Troops

JUNE 24, 1783

As the war inched toward its end, encampments dissolved and the army consolidated at West Point.

Bob, still wearing his cord of recognition under his sleeve, continued his duties. But something within him had changed. He was no longer just a soldier or an orderly, he was a witness to history, and that, he knew, was an honor beyond measure.

However, his thoughts were consumed as to what was to become of him once the army was disbanded. Going back to Middleborough was out of the question. Where could he go? Little did Bob know his greatest battle lay ahead.

June 24th, 1783, dawned heavy with heat and tension, the humid air of Philadelphia thick with unrest. From the upper floors of the State House, Elias Boudinot, President of Congress, stared out at the street below, his face drawn and pale.

The cobblestones thundered with the march of three hundred Pennsylvania Line soldiers, bayonets fixed, drums pounding like war itself had returned. The mutinous veterans encircled the State House, forming a living barricade. They posted sentries at every door, trapping the nation's fragile Congress inside.

Boudinot turned sharply to a trembling clerk. "Send word to General Washington immediately. Congress is under siege."

The clerk ran without a word. Inside the chamber, murmurs spread like wildfire. These were not looters or rabble; these were soldiers. Men who had bled for liberty. But now they were starving, unpaid, and furious. Their message was stark and final: "We will not accept your furloughs. We demand a settlement."

By midday, the decision was made. Congress would not yield to bayonets. Instead, they would flee. By evening, the carriages were packed, and the nation's leaders slipped out under cover of darkness, bound for Princeton, New Jersey, leaving Philadelphia to the mercy of its abandoned warriors.

Far to the north, at West Point, the remnants of the Continental Army dwindled. Of 2,760 men, barely 1,753 were fit for duty. Most of the New England regiments, including Solomon Beebe's, had already marched home, unpaid but proud. The only ones left were the three-year men, the final recruits, which included Bob Shurtlieff.

One week later, on July 1st, the messenger from Philadelphia arrived at West Point and was ushered in without delay into General Washington's quarters.

Inside, Washington sat at his oak desk, quill in hand, working through a clutter of correspondence. The knock at the door brought his head up sharply. "Enter."

Tench Tilghman stepped in, face taut. "Urgent dispatch from President Boudinot, sir."

Washington took it and read in silence.

"Outrageous," he thundered. "This is an insult to every principle we've fought for. Get Generals Knox, Howe, and Paterson here, now."

Tilghman was gone before the echoes of Washington's voice had faded. Within minutes, the three generals stood before him.

"They've surrounded Congress," Washington said. "This cannot stand. I want you to take three regiments, men whose loyalty is unshakable. You'll march for Philadelphia without delay."

Knox gave a curt nod. "We'll leave at dawn."

"No mistakes," Washington warned. "We must remind them what discipline means."

Later that afternoon, in the thinning camp at West Point, Bob was polishing the general's boots when General Paterson approached.

"Shurtlieff, inside."

Bob followed, boots in hand.

"There's trouble with the troops," Paterson said without preamble. "Philadelphia's in chaos. Soldiers from the Pennsylvania Line marched on Congress over back pay. Washington's furious. We leave at dawn."

Bob's pulse quickened, a real march, a mission.

But Paterson shook his head. "You're staying. Four officers, who are imperative for this mission, will arrive in four days. You're to explain the situation and escort them to Philadelphia. Make sure they don't dawdle."

"Understood, sir," Bob said, though disappointed.

Paterson looked him over. "Good. Pack my kit. The city's also battling a plague. If I can avoid it, I'll be out before it catches me."

Bob nodded and got to work. Packing the general's gear was no easy feat. Tents, trunks, field desk, spare boots, uniforms, and all manner of supplies. He worked until midnight before collapsing into bed.

At dawn, the call to arms split the silence. Bob watched as the wagons rolled out. Generals Knox, Howe, and Paterson led the march, trailed by fifteen hundred of the last true soldiers of the Revolution.

Bob stood alone as they vanished down the road. He whispered a prayer for their safe return.

The march south was grueling. The summer heat pressing like a smothering hand. But by the time the troops reached Philadelphia, the streets had quieted. The mutiny had collapsed less than twenty-four hours after it began. The soldiers, still loyal to their officers, accepted a compromise: half-pay now, the rest in certificates. The rebellion had died before the army had even left West Point.

Still, Boudinot insisted that the troops remain. On July 1st, the very day the first dispatch reached Washington, Boudinot sent another dispatch, this time from Princeton, requesting a continued military presence in Philadelphia. The symbolism of order was as necessary as the force itself. So, Paterson, Knox, and Howe camped outside the city, a silent show of stability.

Four days after the troops left West Point, Bob heard hoofbeats echoing up the road. Four riders emerged from the trees.

Bob was sitting on the porch of General Paterson's quarters. He stood as the lead rider reined in his horse.

"You Shurtlieff?"

"Yes, sir," Bob replied.

"I'm Colonel Mercer. With me are Captain Graves, Lieutenant Bellamy, and Major Alden."

Each officer returned Bob's salute.

"We're to report to General Paterson for orders," said Mercer.

"General Paterson's away in Philadelphia. I'm his orderly. A mutiny broke out among the Pennsylvania Line. Your orders are to go there immediately. I'll be going with you."

"How long to Philadelphia?" Mercer asked.

"Five to seven days, depending on our pace."

Graves groaned, stretching stiff arms. "I thought we were here to be discharged, not given new orders."

"General Paterson left four days ago. He expects you to move fast."

"Of course he does," Bellamy muttered.

"General Washington is on post and has sent you an invitation to join him for dinner," said Bob. "You'll be staying at the officer's quarters, where I'll meet you at 7:00 a.m. in the morning with fresh horses and supplies for the journey."

They rode off toward their lodgings, Mercer waving lazily. "We'll be ready."

"Efficient," Bellamy muttered. "I like him."

Bob heard but said nothing. His only concern was to get them south as quickly as possible.

That night, he inspected the horses and double-checked all the supplies. At first light, reveille sounded across camp. Bob knocked on their door.

The four officers emerged, groggy and reluctant.

"Do we really have to leave so soon?" Bellamy groaned.

"Unless you'd prefer a court martial," Mercer said dryly.

Already astride True Briton, Bob said, "Philadelphia awaits, sirs."

They rode east to the ferry, then south down the Albany Post Road.

What should have been a swift weeklong journey stretched into nine days. In every town, prominent families offered food, beds, and brandy. Graves charmed hostesses with stories of valor. Alden sought out every tavern. Bellamy was fawned over wherever they stopped. Mercer let it all unfold with indulgent silence.

Bob, increasingly annoyed, kept them moving as best he could.

CHAPTER 20

Left For Dead

JULY 9, 1783

After nine long days in the saddle, Philadelphia finally shimmered on the horizon like a mirage. For Bob Shurtlieff, the sight stirred something primal. This was the city of revolution where a whole new form of governance had taken root. Never in history had any land dared to forge a republic like this, raw, unfinished, but brimming with untold greatness. A nation not of kings, but of men.

Yet the city was eerily subdued, blanketed in a hush that clashed with Bob's expectations. No fanfare greeted their arrival, just the weary silence of a war ended but not yet finished. Bob and the officers rode to the encampment outside the city, where they reported to General Paterson.

The news struck like a hammer; their journey had been in vain.

After the formalities, Paterson turned to Bob with a wry look.

"You took your time getting here, Shurtlieff. Road give you trouble?"

Bob straightened, a faint, easy smile tugging at his mouth.

"Aye, sir. Not the road so much as the people along it. Every village turned out with food and a place to sleep. Hardly a mile passed without someone pressing bread or cider into our hands. Kindness can wear a man out as quick as marching."

Paterson's brow lifted, his lips twitching at the corners. "Providence favors you then."

"Or sheer stubbornness," Bob said lightly, his smile warming. "Either way, I'm glad to be here."

Paterson gave a short grunt of approval. "Good to have you back."

Later, Bob led True Briton to the stables. A boy was mucking out the stalls, his face smudged but cheerful.

"Good day," Bob greeted. "I'm Bob Shurtlieff. This is True Briton. And you are?"

The lad straightened hastily. "Jimmy Smith, sir."

"No sir about it. Just Bob." He extended his hand. "Pleasure to meet you."

Bob stroked the stallion's neck. "This fellow was once the fastest horse in America. He means the world to me. I need someone I can trust to exercise him when duty calls me elsewhere. Could you manage that?"

Jimmy's eyes gleamed. "Absolutely. He's a beautiful bay."

Bob chuckled. "Perhaps that's what we should call him. Beautiful Bay."

Jimmy laughed. "I'll take care of him like he's my own."

Over the weeks that followed, the bond between Jimmy and True Briton flourished, and so too did the friendship between Jimmy and Bob. They spent long afternoons riding along quiet trails, sharing hopes, stories, and the occasional mischief. In Jimmy, Bob found rare kinship, a confidant in an army that demanded silence and secrecy.

But beneath that peace, danger stirred. Philadelphia throbbed with tension. General Paterson oversaw grim trials, two sergeants sentenced to hang, four privates flogged for mutiny. A new threat crept silently, measles. Unlike smallpox, against which Washington had ordered inoculations, this disease had no defense. Fear rippled through the ranks. General Howe imposed quarantines. The sick were exiled to isolation.

Then, on September 3rd, General Washington's orders came to disband the camp. Discharges were signed. Soldiers returned home with empty pockets and broken bodies. Bob remained among a core group heading back to West Point.

On September 15th, the day before the army's departure back to West Point, the sickness hit. It started with a fever, then a choking cough. Bob tried to shake it off but the illness was merciless. At midday, he was upright outside Paterson's tent. By sunset, he collapsed.

Paterson burst from his tent and saw Bob lying unconscious on the ground. "Shurtlieff!" Two sentries were standing nearby. "You men. Fetch a cart, now! Get him to the hospital as fast as you can! Stay with him until you get a report on his condition and inform me immediately."

The soldiers laid Bob on the cart. Then they began to pull it along the road to the hospital, a mile away from the camp. They finally reached the old Quaker almshouse which had been pressed into service as a hospital. The army had leased it months before when they arrived in Philadelphia. It was needed to house all the sick and dying soldiers who had succumbed to the plague of measles and smallpox ravaging the city.

One of the soldiers spoke to a passing nurse. "This is Bob Shurtlieff, an army Ranger. He reports directly to General Paterson. Please, check him now. We need a report on his condition. The general is waiting."

The nurse, Rosanna Jones, pressed her fingers to Bob's neck, then to his wrist. "No pulse," she said. "He's gone. Move his body to the cart bound for Potter's Field. Down the corridor, end of the hall."

The two men carried Bob's body to the cart and hoisted him on top of a pile of bodies waiting to be taken to the burial field.

But Deborah Sampson, buried beneath Bob's uniform, was not gone. She floated in velvet-dark peace, drifting toward a light so pure it burned with love. From it stepped a radiant figure, wrapped in a light that pulsed with love. Familiar. Eternal.

"Come," He said.

"Jesus?" she whispered.

"Your journey is not finished," He told her. "You will light the path for others. But now you must return."

"No. Please... I want to stay here with You."

"Not yet," He said.

Then, the world yanked her back.

From the cart of corpses came a sudden, low gurgle. Nurse Jones froze midstep, then spun around and felt Bob's hand. It was still warm. She dashed for the doctor.

"Dr. Binney! One of the soldiers for burial, he's still alive!"

Binney looked from a distance. "He's gone," he said flatly.

But she refused to give up. Again, she felt for his pulse.

"Please, Doctor, come back!"

This time, Binney listened. He unbuttoned the jacket and put his hand on Bob's chest to feel for a heartbeat. That's when he discovered the bindings and stepped back in shock.

"Dear God," he whispered. "This soldier is a woman and a Ranger, no less. Go get Matron Parker."

Nurse Jones returned moments later with Matron Parker.

"We have a situation here Matron. This soldier is a woman. We need to put her somewhere safe where her secret will remain protected."

"My apartment is secure," Matron Parker offered.

"Shall we inform the General?" Nurse Jones asked.

"No. Not until we know she'll survive. This scandal could tear through the Army. Move her quietly."

That night, under cover of darkness, Deborah Sampson was carried not to a grave—but into a sanctuary, her secret guarded by two women and a doctor who understood the cost of silence.

CHAPTER 21

Road To Recovery

SEPTEMBER 18, 1783

Deborah stirred, her consciousness creeping back slowly. Sunlight filtered through the window, soft and golden, warming her cheeks. She blinked against the light, disoriented. Panic surged as her hand flew to her chest—her shirt lay open at the neck, her bindings gone. She bolted upright. Pain lanced through her skull, and the world tilted sideways.

"Easy now," came a calm, reassuring voice nearby.

Deborah turned her head slowly. A woman she didn't recognize sat beside her, calm as still water.

"I'm Matron Parker," she said gently, offering a steady smile. "You've been moved to my apartment so I can care for you myself. You've been unconscious for three days."

"My bindings," Deborah whispered anxiously.

"I removed them to help you breathe," the matron said. "And I moved you here to ensure your secret remains protected."

Deborah looked deeply into her eyes, relief washing over her, despite lingering uncertainty. "Thank you," she murmured, her voice barely audible.

"Do you mind telling me your real name, or shall I call you Bob?" asked Matron.

"I prefer Bob. But my real name is Deborah Sampson."

"It's a pleasure to meet you, Bob."

"Does General Paterson know?"

"Nurse Jones declared you dead to the two soldiers who brought you to the hospital. You can imagine her shock when she found you still breathing on a pile of dead bodies waiting to be buried in Potter's field. As I wasn't sure you were going to live, I waited to send word. However, General Paterson left the next day before I could let him know you were still alive."

"So, what you're saying is General Paterson thinks I'm dead."

Matron nodded her head.

"So, where does that leave me?"

"I think that's up to you," said Matron.

Days slipped gently by, each bringing Bob a little more strength, a little more clarity under Matron Parker's nurturing vigilance. Yet with every returning ounce of strength came the gnawing anxiety about his future and what was to become of him.

One quiet afternoon, Matron Parker entered Bob's small sunlit room with a purposeful yet reassuring air.

"Bob, it's time for you to meet Dr. Binney. He needs to see for himself how well you've recovered."

Bob stiffened. "But Matron... won't he discover my secret?"

Matron Parker stepped closer, gently touching Bob's hand, her voice firm yet comforting. "You must trust me, Bob. Dr. Binney will only speak with you. He will not examine you closely or touch your chest."

Bob took a deep breath. "Very well, Matron. I trust you."

Minutes later, Matron Parker guided Bob carefully into a small office tucked away behind the lobby in the hospital.

"Bob, this is Dr. Binney," Matron Parker said softly, stepping back discreetly.

Bob straightened instinctively, forcing calm into his trembling limbs. "Good afternoon, Doctor," he said.

Dr. Binney approached, his warm smile immediately easing some of the tension knotting Bob's shoulders. "Hello, Bob. It's wonderful to see how much you've improved," he said, genuine warmth filling his voice.

"Thank you, Doctor," Bob responded cautiously.

Dr. Binney regarded him thoughtfully for a moment, noting the improved color in his cheeks and the steadiness of his stance. "You look remarkably better," he said approvingly.

Matron Parker spoke up gently from beside them. "Still, he needs careful rest and close medical supervision for at least two more weeks."

Dr. Binney nodded thoughtfully. "That presents something of a dilemma. You see, Bob, you're the last soldier to be treated in this hospital. The army has gone back to West Point, and they have canceled their lease on this building, which belongs to the Quakers. But I have a solution. I'd like you to come and stay with my family as a welcome guest. My wife is a skilled nurse, and Matron Parker lives close by. You'll receive the very best of care while you continue your recovery."

Bob hesitated, emotions swirling rapidly within him, relief and gratitude mingled with lingering apprehension. Yet Dr. Binney's sincerity was unmistakable, and his eyes held nothing but kindness. At last, Bob nodded gratefully. "That would be an honor, Doctor. I thank you for your generosity."

Dr. Binney's smile widened warmly, his nod of acknowledgment comforting and reassuring. "Excellent. Matron Parker will arrange everything. We'll bring you home tomorrow."

The following days at Dr. Binney's home passed swiftly, filled with genuine kindness, warmth, and silent understanding. Bob's strength and spirits rose with each passing day. One bright morning, he was overwhelmed with the urge to see his friend Jimmy at the stables and to find out what happened to True Briton.

At the far end of the stable, Jimmy stood beside True Briton, working the brush over the stallion's sleek, bay colored hide. The horse flicked his ears and lifted his head sharply, as if sensing something in the air. Then, with a deep, knowing whinny, he turned, his large, intelligent eyes and looked directly at Bob.

"Bob?" Jimmy's voice cracked with disbelief. "You're alive! The soldiers said you were dead. I told True Briton…" His gaze dropped briefly to the horse, his voice thick with emotion. "We both thought we'd lost you."

Bob's lips curved into a soft, warm smile, though his throat tightened at the sight of them. "I nearly was," he admitted. "Matron Parker kept me from slipping away."

Jimmy shook his head in amazement. "Well, True Briton and I are grateful for that."

Bob's eyes drifted over the stallion, his fingers itching to touch him, to reassure himself he was real. "I'm surprised he's still here."

"I think they just forgot about him, plain and simple," Jimmy said with a wry chuckle. "But I didn't. I've been looking after him, just like you told me to."

Bob's chest tightened with gratitude as he reached out, running a hand over True Briton's velvety muzzle. The stallion huffed softly, pressing his warm nose into his palm, as if to say he hadn't forgotten him either. "Thank you, Jimmy," he murmured. "I thought I'd lost him forever."

"Most of the men have been discharged," Jimmy said, glancing toward the empty stalls. "Only a handful went back to West Point with General Paterson. So where does that leave you?"

Bob kept his hand on True Briton's neck, feeling the steady rise and fall of his breath. "I'll be heading back soon," he said quietly. "I signed on for three years, and my service isn't finished yet." His fingers absently stroking the horse's mane. "Besides, if trouble ever returns, they'll need soldiers who still remember how to fight."

Jimmy nodded. "I suppose they will."

They stood there in the golden light, the past and present weaving between them. And as the afternoon stretched on, they talked, of battles and homecomings, of the lives they had left behind and the uncertain paths ahead. For now, at least, they had this moment, and the warmth of old friendship to steady them.

A week later, Bob sat comfortably in an armchair, grasping a quill pen as he wrote in his journal. He had documented all his adventures since he joined the army, making sure he remembered things as they happened and not just his imaginings.

His thoughts drifted towards an uncertain future, wondering what was to become of him.

Dr. Binney stepped into the room, an envelope clutched tightly in his hand.

"Bob, you're strong enough now," Binney said, stepping closer. "It's time for you to return to West Point. General Paterson will want to see you." He handed Bob the envelope. "You'll deliver this to him personally."

A chill that had nothing to do with the air prickled down Bob's spine. The letter, a simple task on the surface, yet it throbbed with an unspoken significance. And then he met Dr. Binney's gaze.

Bob was hit with the sudden realization that Dr. Binney knew. He had always known. And yet, even now, Binney allowed Deborah's masquerade as Bob Shurtlieff to continue. And so would she, until forced to give it up.

"I'll deliver it," Bob said.

Dr. Binney's smile was small but full of understanding, of unspoken truths that neither of them needed to voice. "I trust you will."

Bob extended his hand. "Thank you for everything."

"Safe travels, Bob," Binney said. And then he added, "You're a fine soldier. General Paterson will be pleased to see you again."

Packing was swift. Bob shouldered his knapsack with practiced ease, bidding farewell to Dr. and Mrs. Binney, and their two bright-eyed children.

Then, he was off to the stables. True Briton's ears flicked at his approach. Jimmy looked up from where he was mucking a stall, his face breaking into a grin.

"Hey there, Bob. Heading out?"

"Back to West Point."

Jimmy's smile faltered. "Man. I sure hate to see you both go."

Bob smiled. "Duty calls."

"Alright then. I'll get him saddled up for you."

The silence stretched between them as Jimmy worked. When at last Bob swung into the saddle, Jimmy stepped back, his arms folded tight across his chest.

Jimmy sighed. "You take care of yourself."

"You too," Bob said with a smile.

And then, with a click of his tongue, Bob urged True Briton forward. The great horse moved beneath him, strong and sure. The wind picked up as they rode out into the morning light.

Jimmy stood watching, blinking hard against the tears in his eyes, as Bob and True Briton rode out of his life forever.

CHAPTER 22

The River and the Reckoning

OCTOBER 19, 1783

Bob eased back on True Briton's reins as the trail opened onto the banks of the Hudson. Rain clouds swelled on the horizon, ominous, black, and ready to burst.

"That sky doesn't look good," Bob muttered, his voice barely rising above the wind.

The ferryman waved them forward, urgency in his tone. "Storm's comin' hard. If you're goin', go now."

Bob nodded once, urging True Briton forward. The great stallion's hooves thudded against the wooden planks as the boat rocked beneath them. Passengers clutched their belongings, whispering anxious prayers. Overhead, the wind began to howl.

They had only reached the halfway point when the ferryman shouted, "Hold tight!" His voice cracked with panic. "Brace yourselves!"

A bolt of lightning split the sky and struck the mast with a crack like cannon fire.

Bob turned—too late.

A jagged beam came crashing down, slamming into his skull. The world vanished in white-hot pain before he slipped into the void.

Bob fell—and the river rose to meet him.

His knapsack vanished into the deep, taking everything he owned: his money, his clothes, his journal—every word he had written. The ferry lurched violently, then capsized. Screams disappeared into the storm as bodies and belongings tumbled overboard into chaos.

Bob sank. But True Briton did not.

The stallion kicked and thrashed, teeth latching onto Bob's sodden shirt. With every ounce of strength, the horse swam—through wind, through current, through hell itself—dragging the limp figure of Bob in his jaws like a fallen foal.

"Over here!" voices shouted through the rain.

A wiry, broad-shouldered man darted down the muddy bank and plunged into the tide. With strong arms and calloused hands, he hauled Bob from the river and rolled him onto his side.

Bob gasped, vomiting water, lungs convulsing as life clawed its way back into his body.

"Easy, mister. I got you now. Name's Caleb."

"Bob... Shurtlieff," he rasped, teeth chattering.

Caleb studied him. "Heard that name before. Gimme a minute—it'll come to me."

Bob blinked against the rain. "What happened?"

"You lived, is what happened," Caleb said. "Ferry went under. Half the folks on it are dead. That horse of yours dragged you out of the water, nearly drowned himself doing it."

"True Briton saved me?"

"Ain't never seen nothin' like it. Come on now, let's get you warm. My cabin's a ways from here. Do you feel up to riding your horse, to save your strength?"

Bob shivered violently but nodded. "Yes."

He climbed into the saddle, his body trembling but grateful for the animal's strength beneath him.

The fire in Caleb's hearth crackled with life, casting a warm orange glow over the simple cabin. Bob sat wrapped in a thick, story-laced quilt, hands curled around a steaming mug of coffee. Outside the door, True Briton stood like a sentinel.

Caleb nodded toward the horse. "That animal's more than muscle and hide. He pulled you from the deep like he knew your life mattered. That ain't luck. That's Gods's Mercy."

Bob's eyes misted over as he glanced toward True Briton, heart swelling with gratitude. "Thank God he got left behind by the army in Philadelphia," he whispered softly, "not many people can say their horse saved their life."

Caleb smiled, sitting back in his chair. "I reckon he's as loyal a friend as a man could ask for."

"He's even better. He never criticizes or complains, which is more than I can say for most friends."

"Caleb laughed, then paused, eyes sharpening. "Bob Shurtlieff... now I remember. My cousin George talked about you. Said you offered him freedom once. He turned you down. Stayed with Widow Hunt. Said she treated him more like a friend than a slave. Didn't see no better place to go."

Bob nodded, heart aching. "Freedom means different things to different people, I suppose."

"It sure do," Caleb agreed. "Sometimes it's a place. Sometimes it's a person. Sometimes it's a story buried deep in your soul."

Bob looked at the intricate details on the quilt covering him. "I've never seen a quilt quite like this. It looks almost like a map. I recognize some of these landmarks."

Caleb shifted nervously and explained, "My mother made it from her memories of our home in Africa. She sewed it into fabric so she'd never forget."

"Well, I guess I was mistaken about the landmarks," Bob replied. "Your mother is very talented. It's a lovely quilt and could even be hung on the wall as a fine work of art."

"Thank you. She's gone now, but her story lives on in this quilt," said Caleb.

The next morning broke clear and golden, the river now calm and indifferent, as though it hadn't tried to kill him the day before.

Bob mounted True Briton, head pounding but heart steadier. "Thank you, Caleb. I owe you more than I can say."

Caleb grinned. "Just keep goin', Bob Shurtlieff. I reckon there's a lot more ahead for you than behind."

The gates of West Point loomed ahead through the haze. Bob shook his head in disbelief at how he lost his rucksack with all that he owned when the ferry capsized, except for Dr. Binney's fateful letter, which he kept in a worn leather wallet in a pocket on the inside of his coat. He could have thrown it away. But it was a matter of his own personal integrity. He would deliver it as promised, despite the consequences.

He dismounted before General Paterson's quarters. "Good afternoon. I'm Bob Shurtlieff, reporting for duty. Could you let General Paterson know I've arrived?"

Before the orderly could answer, the door swung open, revealing the stunned face of General Paterson. "My God, Shurtlieff! They told us you were dead!" The general stepped forward, stunned disbelief softening into astonishment and relief.

Bob summoned a weary smile. "Thankfully, not yet, sir. Measles, pneumonia, even a shipwreck on the Hudson River, couldn't kill me. Seems Heaven itself wasn't ready to claim me."

Paterson shook his head slowly, astonishment mingling with concern. "Come inside, Shurtlieff," he urged gently, grasping Bob's shoulder.

In the sanctuary of the general's office, Bob silently withdrew the worn red Moroccan wallet from inside his coat. With trembling hands, he handed the sealed letter to Paterson.

"From Dr. Binney, sir," Bob whispered hoarsely, "I'll leave you to read it in private."

Bob turned and slipped from the room, leaning against the cool hallway wall, his heart pounding ferociously in his chest. He closed his eyes, saying a desperate prayer from the depths of his soul.

Please, God, he prayed. *Let him show me mercy. Don't let my masquerade be all he sees. Let him remember my courage, my loyalty. Let that count for something. Amen.*

The silence stretched unbearably until he heard Paterson's steady voice calling him back. Gathering every scrap of courage left, Bob stepped inside, his heart suspended between hope and despair.

The general stood near his desk, eyes locked onto Bob, the letter trembling slightly in his grip.

"Shurtlieff, is it true that beneath your uniform you carry the identity of a woman?"

Deborah's breath caught in her throat. Fear surged. Instinctively, she sank to her knees under the weight of dread.

"General," she pleaded desperately, her eyes filled with tears. "What fate awaits me if I say yes?"

"Shurtlieff," he murmured gently, stepping forward and placing a comforting hand upon Deborah's shoulder, "no harm will befall you here. You are under my protection."

The general's voice swelled with passionate sincerity. He helped her stand up. "Do you realize the enormity of your achievements? Your company was the best, a force feared and respected throughout the army. Yet even among such remarkable men, you shone brightest. You outshot, outfought, outmarched, and outlasted our finest," Paterson continued.

"And you did so carrying a truth no one could have imagined. That is courage in its purest form."

Deborah lifted her eyes. "You honor me, sir, but will others not scorn me for the deception?"

"They will follow my lead," Paterson said. "You're not a scandal. You're a legacy."

"What happens to me now, sir?" she asked, still trembling.

"I'll speak to Generals Washington and Knox about how to discreetly handle your discharge," he replied, smiling.

Deborah's voice cracked. "General, I've nowhere to go. Even though I'll be discharged, may I remain here under your command, at least until I figure things out?"

Paterson's response was immediate and decisive. "Your quarters and duties await you, Shurtlieff. You're welcome to stay, unless I hear otherwise." His eyes softened again. "But first, sit with me. Share your story, your real name, and the motive that drove you to accomplish what few could even imagine."

Overwhelmed, yet deeply moved, Deborah sank into the chair, a profound relief easing the haunting pangs of fear and secrecy. Slowly, with quiet dignity, she began to tell the story that had shaped her extraordinary journey.

CHAPTER 23

A Surge Of Pride

OCTOBER 25, 1783

Deborah Sampson, still known to all but a trusted few as Bob Shurtlieff, moved silently through her daily duties under General Paterson's scrutiny. The General, an honorable man, bound tightly by discretion, continued firmly addressing her as Shurtlieff, safeguarding her secret from the relentless tongues of idle gossip.

On the brisk morning of October 25th, 1783, Deborah's pulse quickened as General Paterson's commanding voice thundered through the doorway. "Shurtlieff! Step inside."

She squared her shoulders and entered confidently. "Yes, General."

"I've spoken with Generals Washington and Knox about your situation. You'll be officially discharged today but will remain under my command until we march triumphantly into New York City on Evacuation Day on November 25th.

There will be a grand parade marking our final victory over the British. You've earned your place among us, Shurtlieff. With your courage, your discipline, and your unimpeachable record, it is only fitting that you march among us when we reclaim our city."

A surge of pride and bittersweet joy welled up in Deborah's heart. "Thank you, sir, for this great honor."

"And afterward? Will you return to Massachusetts, to your mother?" he asked.

"I'll return to Massachusetts, General, but not to my mother. She would never let me forget my transgressions. The humiliation, as she sees it, of me rejecting her chosen husband, compounded by the unforgivable sin of living my life as a soldier, I'd never hear the end of it. Besides, she'd swiftly try to arrange another marriage, hoping to sell me off again.

"Have you any other options?"

"I've a cousin in Sharon, a good man who could probably use another hand on his farm. I'll seek refuge there until I can reclaim my independence. I was once a fine weaver and spinner and I know my way around a schoolroom."

Paterson's nod was filled with respect. "An excellent plan, Shurtlieff. Now, report to General Knox, your discharge awaits."

"Yes, sir." Deborah saluted sharply and strode out.

Approaching General Knox's quarters, Deborah spotted Lt. Colonel Tilghman. When he saw her, his face broke into a wide smile.

"Ah, Shurtlieff! Just the person I was hoping to see."

"Good morning, Colonel." Deborah returned his greeting with a crisp salute.

"At ease," he chuckled warmly. "I've just spoken with Knox. He oversees dispersing surplus army property, including True Briton. I intended to purchase him myself, but fate intervened. He's already been sold to a man named Justin Morgan, who plans to breed a new line of intelligent, strong and fast American horses, the Morgan horse."

"True Briton deserves such a legacy," she said.

"Indeed, he does," Tilghman agreed fervently. "He must be delivered to Morgan in West Springfield, Massachusetts. I'll ride him one last time during our victory parade. Afterward, would you take him north? I assume you're heading to Massachusetts anyway, aren't you?"

"I'd be honored, Colonel. He's become more than a companion; he's my truest friend. I'll see him safely to his new owner."

Tilghman's voice softened with admiration. "Remarkable creature, isn't he? The finest horse I've ever ridden."

"He saved my life," Deborah confessed.

Tilghman's eyes widened in astonishment. "How so?"

Deborah steadied herself, recalling vividly that harrowing moment. "We were crossing the Hudson when a violent storm overturned our ferry. A falling mast struck me senseless, sending me underwater. True Briton, fell in on top of me. By some miracle, he seized my coat between his teeth and swam back to shore with me, unconscious and dangling like a rag doll, from his mouth."

"Extraordinary!" Tilghman breathed, his eyes gleaming with wonder. "I've never known a horse capable of such bravery."

Deborah smiled. "He was accidentally left behind when the troops left Philadelphia. It's as if Providence marked him precisely for my rescue."

Tilghman regarded her solemnly. "Providence indeed, Shurtlieff—Providence, and the noblest horse I've ever known."

"I can assure you, Colonel," Deborah said, voice firm with determination, "I'll deliver him safely to Mr. Morgan."

Then, turning to the task at hand, she approached Knox's orderly. "I'm Bob Shurtlieff. I've come for my discharge papers."

"Wait here. I'll check with General Knox to see if they're ready," the orderly replied.

Deborah stood in quiet contemplation. She marveled at how far she'd traveled—not just in miles, but in the shedding of skin, in the building of muscle, in the quiet, gritted persistence that turned a girl into a warrior. She whispered a fervent prayer of thanks, acknowledging the Lord's mercy and grace that had sustained her on this challenging journey.

The orderly returned without her papers. "The General wishes to see you, Shurtlieff."

She entered briskly, saluting General Knox, who looked up with a mixture of curiosity and assessment. "I don't usually meet discharging soldiers in person," he began gruffly. "But General Paterson spoke highly of your exploits. He mentioned your courage and determination. He seemed to think you were something out of the common way."

Deborah stood tall, her posture firm. "I'm no exception. I fought, against all odds, side by side with men whose respect I earned through my actions and bravery."

Knox frowned, his eyes narrowing. "So, you'd have women bearing arms and marching into combat, shoulder to shoulder, with men? The distraction for the men would be disastrous."

"Not just marching beside them—leading!" she replied. "I stand before you, general, a soldier, a Ranger, a woman. I fought, bled, and endured cloaked in secrecy. My record is a testament to what women can accomplish, when freed from prejudice and limitation."

He handed Deborah her papers. "You're now officially discharged from the army." Knox looked away irritably, scowling, "Dismissed."

She turned and walked out, the door clicking shut behind her.

In her hand, she held the proof of what she'd done. But it wasn't the paper that mattered. It was the path that couldn't be erased: the miles walked, the battles fought, and the courage it took to reach this moment.

She hadn't just worn the uniform of a Ranger. She had redefined it.

CHAPTER 24

Evacuation Day

NOVEMBER 25, 1783 – 9:00 A.M.

The morning sun cast long shadows across the city as the British soldiers made their final march toward the East River. Their red coats, once symbols of power, were now worn as a testament to the end of an empire.

Sir Guy Carleton, the British Commander-in-Chief for North America, was already aboard HMS Ceres, anchored off Staten Island. His officers led the column of the remaining soldiers with rigid faces, burdened by the weight of defeat. Carleton had done his duty, overseeing the evacuation of thousands of Loyalists, British troops, and Black slaves, who had fought for Britain, ensuring their safe passage away from the newborn nation.

In Harlem, the Continental Army remained camped, awaiting the final departure of the British. General Paterson had one last assignment.

"Shurtlieff." Paterson's voice carried the authority of command, but there was something else beneath it, something warmer. "I've received an order from General Washington. He wants my best Ranger to ride to Fort George and make certain the last of the redcoats have cleared the city before we begin the parade. Also, you're to check the entire parade route and make sure the British haven't left anything behind that might be unacceptable." Paterson continued. "To be honest, you've been discharged, so you could refuse. But tell me, would you take on one last mission for your country?"

"I'm honored you would ask me, sir. Of course I will."

A smile flickered across Paterson's lips. "Good. You'll go in civilian clothes, no uniform, no sword. Just a pistol, and discretion."

She nodded. "Understood."

"You'll need a horse to get there and back in time. Parade begins at one o'clock."

"Would it be alright if I take True Briton?" she asked.

"So long as Tilghman has no objections."

"I'll leave at once."

Within moments, she had changed and gone in search of Lt. Col. Tilghman, finding him in quiet discussion with Washington himself. The urgency of the mission left her no choice, she stepped forward.

"Excuse me, sirs. General Paterson has assigned me to scout the parade route. I need a horse. May I ride True Briton, Colonel?"

Tilghman smiled. "Yes. Just be sure to bring him back without injury, or General Knox will have my hide."

"Your name, soldier?" Washington asked.

"Bob Shurtlieff, sir."

"Ah." A knowing nod. "So, you're the best of our Rangers."

"General Paterson seems to think so."

"And I trust his judgment. The information you bring back will ensure our army's final parade is unchallenged. We don't want any surprises."

Deborah met his gaze, unwavering. "I'll make sure of it, sir."

She turned, striding towards True Briton, who stood tethered nearby.

Washington murmured to Tilghman, "She's extraordinary. Courageous even."

"More than that," Tilghman replied. "She's outshone every man in her company. She's been shot, dug the bullet out herself, rather than reveal her gender, and survived death three times over."

"Who'd have thought a woman could be capable of such things. That's more than most men could do!" said Washington.

After thoroughly checking the route: Bowery, Chatham, then Pearl Street toward Whitehall Slip, Deborah headed to the bustling docks.

The *South Carolina* was one of the last British transport ships in the harbor. Sleek and long, with taut rigging and three towering masts, it was once an elegant American built frigate.

Today, it would be among the last of the crowded British transport ships to get under way.

There was irony in her lines, bitter and rich. She was constructed in Philadelphia in 1780 for the South Carolina Navy, intended to strike fear into British shipping. Based on European designs, once envisioned for the Continental Navy, she was a marvel of American craftsmanship: fast, agile, and armed with forty guns. She was meant to be the pride of the Southern resistance at sea.

But political red tape, infighting, and poor coordination left her isolated. After a brief string of privateering victories, she was cornered off the Delaware Capes in December 1782 by three British warships. She didn't go down in flames—she was taken.

And now, a year later, she sailed under British command, stripped of her American flag and ideals, reduced to a vessel of retreat. It was on this ship, meant once to fight for liberty, that Loyalist families, runaway slaves, and the remaining red-coated soldiers of a defeated empire, made their final escape from American soil.

Just then, amidst the chaos of the wharf, James Delancey appeared with his young and noticeably pregnant wife, seventeen-year-old Martha, threading their way toward the gangway. Behind them trailed his household, a dozen slaves in chains, silently following, bound for exile along with the British, and remaining Loyalists, evacuating New York.

"I don't believe it. Look, Martha," James said, halting abruptly. "There's True Briton."

He veered off course, striding toward the horse. Awe flickered across his face as he reached out to stroke the animal's neck. "Hello, boy!"

"How extraordinary. It's as if he came to say goodbye," Martha said.

James nodded slowly, eyes scanning True Briton with reverence. "What are you doing here boy, on this of all days?"

"I brought him." Deborah stepped forward and gathered up the reins.

Delancey's expression hardened. He stared at her, hatred sparking behind his eyes. "What are you doing here?"

"I came to make sure the British didn't leave any of their rubbish behind," she said. "And True Briton is with me."

Delancey shook his head in disbelief. "What a waste. He's the finest horse I've ever known. What happens to him now?"

Deborah held her ground. "He's going to sire an entirely new intelligent, strong and fast American breed, the Morgan horse. It's the future he deserves. A legacy worthy of his spirit."

For the briefest second, Delancey's sneer faltered. "Well," he said, turning away. "That's better than spending the rest of his life pulling a wagon. He always was meant for greatness."

Without another word, or a backward glance, James and Martha stepped onto the gangway, disappearing into the crowd already on deck.

Just before the final boat shoved off, a distant boom rolled down river. General Knox's American advance guard had entered the city from the Bowery and fired a thirteen-gun salute from Fort George. The cannon thundered in steady rhythm, one shot for each of the thirteen United States. The echoes rolled through the harbor like liberty's reply to tyranny's retreat.

Deborah watched as the crew of the *South Carolina* cast off the final mooring lines. The ship sailed away carrying with her the weight of a vanquished empire.

Deborah stood still for a long moment, eyes on the horizon, then swung into the saddle and turned True Briton northward toward Harlem. Her duty was done. Or so it seemed.

As they passed Fort George, she drew up short. The British flag, the Union Jack, still flew from the flagpole, nailed fast at the top. The halyards were gone. The shaft of the pole had been slathered in axle grease from base to crown, glistening in the morning sun like a cruel joke.

"No," she whispered. Then louder, to no one in particular. "This can't be. If Washington sees this…"

The British had left their final insult behind, a parting gesture meant to humiliate General Washington and mock the cause for which so many had bled and died. And Deborah, who had been charged with preventing exactly this, had failed.

She was still staring up at the pole, fists clenched, when a young sailor appeared at her side. He looked up wordlessly, his eyes following hers. A moment later, another man stepped forward, carrying an American flag.

"What's to be done, then?" the man with the flag asked.

"We have to get it down," Deborah said grimly.

"I'll do it," the sailor said, already stepping forward. "Hand me the flag."

He had no other tools but a hammer and nails in his pocket and the strength in his limbs. One by one, he drove nails into the pole, creating footholds. The grease slicked his grip, and more than once he nearly fell. The higher he climbed, the heavier the nation's hope seemed to rest upon him.

When he reached the summit, he tore the Union Jack from its perch and let it fall to the ground. A heartbeat later, he raised the Stars and Stripes in its place. The wind caught the fabric, and it billowed wide, bold, bright, and defiant.

A roar went up from the watching crowd, cheers, whistles, and cries of triumph. In that final act, the colonies were truly free. The Revolution was, at last, complete.

Deborah rushed to meet the sailor as he descended.

"You've no idea what you've done," she said, grasping his hand. "You've saved the General from disgrace. Saved us all, really."

"That's kind of you to say."

"What's your name?" she asked.

"John Van Arsdale," he said. "And yours?"

"Bob Shurtlieff," she answered. "U.S. Army Ranger. I was sent here to make sure the British didn't leave any last barbs behind. I'll report your name to the General, you can be sure of that. You're a hero today."

Van Arsdale smiled faintly. "Just glad to see that blasted flag gone for good."

"You didn't just tear down a flag," she said. "You raised a nation."

With her mission complete, Deborah turned True Briton and galloped hard for Harlem, her heart pounding with urgency and pride.

When she arrived, the army was already gathering. Troops stood in crisp formation, flags snapping in the cold breeze. Generals Paterson, Washington, and Lt. Col. Tilghman stood together, heads bent in quiet conversation.

Tilghman stepped forward and took True Briton's reins as she dismounted.

"Back just in time," he said with a nod.

With one fluid motion, Tilghman swung into the saddle with practiced ease. "Come to Fraunces Tavern two hours after the parade," he said. "We'll be in the Long Room. I'll tell you where to find True Briton."

"Yes, sir," she replied.

She retrieved her army jacket and cap from her satchel. There was a strange weight to the fabric now—heavier, more solemn. For the last time, she buttoned the coat and settled the cap on her head. Her fingers trembled slightly as she whispered the familiar lines from Ephesians, invoking the Armor of God—truth, righteousness, peace, faith, salvation.

"Armor on," she said aloud.

With that, the drums began. The parade commenced.

Washington rode at the head of the procession, flanked by his officers, their uniforms brilliant beneath the Autumn sun. The streets of New York were alive with celebration, cheering crowds waving flags. From Bowery to Chatham to Broadway, they marched into a city reclaimed.

The American flag above Fort George flew high, but not everyone beneath it was free. Not yet. Not truly. Some still lived in bondage. Others were shackled by the world's expectations, denied the chance to prove who they were and what they could be.

As the Stars and Stripes waved above her, Deborah vowed silently to continue the fight, daring to live life on her own terms as a masterless woman.

CHAPTER 25

The Final Salute

NOVEMBER 25, 1783 – 7:00 P.M.

Fraunces Tavern loomed ahead—brick-red, weathered, scarred by time, but unbowed. Deborah pushed through its heavy oak doors into a world of smoke and warmth. The air was thick with the scent of roasted meat, cider, and the crackle of a fire licking at the hearth.

Behind the bar stood Sam Fraunces, wiping a tankard with calm precision. His sharp eyes landed on her instantly.

"You must be the soldier Tilghman told me to look out for. Shurtlieff, is it?"

Deborah nodded, brushing dust from her sleeve. "I'm here to collect a horse."

He grunted, a sound halfway between a laugh and a sigh. "You'll have to wait. The officers are still upstairs toasting their glory. Have a seat. Are you hungry?"

She shook her head. "I've no coin."

"Tilghman said to feed you whatever you wanted. On him." He turned and walked away before she could object.

The fire from the hearth reached into her bones as she collapsed into a chair. A moment later, a feast was laid before her—roast beef, buttered carrots, crisp potatoes drowning in gravy, warm bread, a tankard of cider, and a slice of hot apple pie steaming in the chill air.

Deborah's stomach clenched at the sight. She hadn't realized how hungry she was until now.

"Go on, then," Fraunces said, crossing his arms as he watched her. "You've earned it, soldier."

She dug in like a starving wolf, tears of bliss stinging her eyes at the first bite. "God in heaven! Thank you."

She glanced around, taking in the sturdy beams, the well-worn floors. "I bet this place has some history behind it."

Fraunces nodded. "Stephen Delancey built it, once a powerful name in this city. Now his grandson sails for Nova Scotia with his slaves, never to return. Imagine—the home of Loyalist nobility, now a sanctuary for the very men who drove them out. Funny how war turns the world upside down."

Deborah exhaled sharply, considering his words. "I saw James Delancey leave today. His slaves didn't have a choice. His family will start again, but what of them?"

"They were never free to begin with," replied Sam as he turned and walked away to check on his other customers.

Minutes later, Sam returned. "Looks like you enjoyed that."

"I sure did. It was the best meal I've ever had," she said, licking her lips.

He studied her. "Where are you headed next?"

"West Springfield, Massachusetts. I'm delivering Tilghman's horse to his new owner."

"And after that?" asked Sam.

She hesitated. "I'm not sure."

He leaned in, voice low and firm. "I've run this tavern a long time. I know when someone's carrying a secret like a stone in their pocket. What's yours, soldier?"

Her spine straightened. "What makes you think I have a secret?"

"Because everyone does," he said. "Tell you what, I'll trade you my secret for yours."

Her brow lifted. "Alright. You first."

A slow grin spread across Sam's face. "Fair enough." He leaned on the bar, lowering his voice. "My ancestors were slaves," he said simply. "Ironically, I pass for white and do business as a white man. I own this place. I serve men who'd have bought my kin. And I do it on my terms. That's my secret."

Deborah nodded, eyes shining. "That is a truth worth honoring."

"And yours?"

She looked down, then met his gaze. "My name is Deborah Sampson. I'm a woman. I've served in Washington's army disguised as a man."

His face didn't flinch. Instead, he gave a small, incredulous smile. "Well, now. That's a tale for the ages."

"You're not surprised?"

"Seen too much to be surprised. You fought. You bled. You survived. That makes you a soldier."

"Thank you," she whispered.

Sam lifted his tankard in salute. "To hidden truths. And to those who dare live them."

The evening stretched on. Deborah found herself drawn into the warm, flickering light of the tavern, listening to Sam's stories, trading pieces of herself in return. But then, the heavy tread of shoes sounded on the stairs. The officers were descending, their laughter rolling ahead of them. Deborah scanned their faces. No Tilghman.

Where was he? She turned, moving quickly up the stairs. As she stepped into the Long Room, she found Tilghman clasping Washington's hand, a final goodbye.

Tilghman turned, spotting her in the doorway. "Ah, Shurtlieff. You'll find True Briton in the stables behind the tavern, saddled up and ready for you."

Before she could thank him, Washington turned to her. No audience. No protocol. Just the man at the center of the Revolution, looking into the eyes of someone who had stood her ground when it mattered most.

"Private Shurtlieff."

Deborah stepped forward. "Yes, sir."

"I've heard of your remarkable achievements," he began. "You have shown immense fortitude, courage and skill that far exceeded your Ranger's training."

"Thank you, sir," she replied. "It's been an honor to serve under your command."

"You did more than serve," he continued. "You endured the worst conditions, took the hardest assignments, and outperformed men whose bravery was unparalleled. And you did it carrying a secret you had to hide every day."

She stepped forward, voice steady and rising. "General, I speak not just for myself, but for every woman who has ever been told she could not, should not, dare not. Courage knows no gender. I never fought to prove a woman could do what a man could. I fought because I must. Because the cause was just, and I was ready."

She held nothing back now—not anger, not grief, just clarity.

"One day," she said, voice steady, "women won't have to bind their bodies or borrow false names to do what I did. They'll serve in their own right—openly, trusted, and valued, not as exceptions, but as equals."

"The courage you speak of," Washington said quietly, "is the kind that shapes nations. Yours is a name that deserves its place in the history of this republic."

Deborah met his gaze—unflinching, resolute. A quiet smile touched her lips.

"From your lips to God's ears, sir. May it be so."

Washington paused, then smiled. His eyes full of respect for the valiant woman standing before him, a soldier, a Ranger, like no other.

"Dismissed, soldier."

Deborah raised her hand and gave her final salute, turned, and walked out as a soldier who had endured, excelled, and changed the course of what's possible—for women to one day serve openly in the military.

Outside, the sky stretched sharp and vast, stars blazing overhead like a thousand eyes—watching, waiting.

Deborah swung onto True Briton with the confidence of a soldier who had earned every scar. The stallion tossed his head, charged and ready.

"Let's ride, boy. We've got one last mission to accomplish. Your legacy awaits."

They rode into the dark, the beat of hooves fading into the hush of stars.

Deborah Sampson—Soldier, Ranger, Woman—slipped the bonds of expectation and thundered into legend.

AUTHOR'S NOTE

This book began, quite unexpectedly, in 2003 when I first discovered the story of Deborah Sampson. From the moment I encountered her, I was struck by her courage, grit, and refusal to live within the boundaries set for her. Here was a young woman who bound her chest, donned a soldier's uniform, and marched into the Revolutionary War. Her story would not let me go. It settled into my heart and stayed there until I knew I had to write it.

As a Navy veteran, I felt a deep kinship with Deborah. I know something of what it means to wear a uniform, to serve, and to defy expectations placed upon women. Writing this novel became not only an act of historical imagination but also a dialogue across centuries between her experience and my own.

Deborah Sampson is recognized as America's first female veteran and the first woman to receive a military pension for her combat service—thanks in no small part to Paul Revere's advocacy on her behalf. Her bravery on the battlefield and her relentless fight for recognition echo across centuries, resonating especially with women who have worn the uniform and fought, in every sense of the word, to be seen.

Though written as a novel, this book is firmly grounded in fact. Every effort has been made to follow the arc of Deborah's life as faithfully as possible, relying on primary sources, historical documents, and scholarly research to capture the world in which she lived and served.

I am especially indebted to Alfred F. Young's groundbreaking work, *Masquerade*. Of all the books written about Deborah Sampson, his remains the most meticulous, accurate, and illuminating. It became the foundation on which I built this narrative, guiding me to remain true to the known record while allowing space to imagine the silences in her story.

The details of Deborah's service—her enlistment as Robert Shurtlieff, her injuries, her time in hospital, and her honorable discharge—are all grounded in documented fact. Likewise, the events surrounding the evacuation of New York and the fate of True Briton, the horse who became the foundation sire of the Morgan breed, are rooted in history.

Where history offers no voice, I have used fiction to imagine Deborah's inner world and the private words of Washington, Paterson, Knox, Tilghman, and others. Fictional characters such as Toby Granger, serve as bridges, illuminating themes of loyalty, freedom, and identity during an age of upheaval.

I believe that fiction, responsibly written, can illuminate the past as vividly as any textbook. My aim has been to remain faithful to the essence of Deborah Sampson's story: her bravery, her resilience, and her defiance of expectation. Everything imagined here has been done with respect for the facts.

Across the centuries, the inspiring story of Deborah Sampson reminds us that courage knows no gender.

ABOUT PAT PATTEN

Patricia "Grandma Pat" Patten is a Navy veteran, writer, and debut novelist whose passion for uncovering untold stories drives her work. At seventy-five, she has transformed decades of research and imagination into *Between War and Peace*, a sweeping historical novel that reimagines the Revolutionary War through the eyes of Deborah Sampson—the fearless woman who disguised herself as a man to fight in the Continental Army's elite Ranger Special Forces unit.

Beyond the page, Pat sees her writing as a ministry, an invitation to explore faith, courage, and the resilience of the human spirit. A portion of proceeds from her book is dedicated to supporting female veteran organizations, raising awareness for women who have served and sacrificed.

When she's not writing, Pat enjoys exploring new technology, cooking healthy meals, and playing board games. She lives in Jacksonville, Florida, where she continues to write, speak, and advocate for stories that remind us that courage knows no gender.

JOIN PAT ON HER SOCIAL MEDIA

Facebook	Pat Patten – Author
LinkedIn	Pat Patten
TikTok	@pattenspoint
Substack	@patpatten
Amazon Author Page	Pat-Patten
YouTube	@PattensPoint